CHRISTMAS AT CASTLE ELRICK

Severely injured in the Napoleonic Wars, Sir Ralph Elrick has been brooding in his castle for years, waiting for Miss Verity Sanderson to reach her majority and marry him. The week before Christmas, she sets off to his ancestral home to become his wife. But Castle Elrick is a cold, unwelcoming place — and Ralph and his small staff are not the only residents. Will Christmas be a joyous celebration, or will the ghosts of Castle Elrick force the newlyweds apart?

FENELLA J. MILLER

CHRISTMAS AT CASTLE ELRICK

Complete and Unabridged

LINFORD
Leicester

First published in Great Britain in 2017

First Linford Edition
published 2017

A catalogue record for this book is available
from the British Library.

ISBN 978–1–4448–3403–1

Published by
F. A. Thorpe (Publishing)
Anstey, Leicestershire

Set by Words & Graphics Ltd.
Anstey, Leicestershire
Printed and bound in Great Britain by
T. J. International Ltd., Padstow, Cornwall

This book is printed on acid-free paper

This book is for my wonderful
daughter-in-law
Karyn Miller

1

Verity stared at the letter her mother had just handed her, hardly able to comprehend the enormity of the contents. 'Mama, is this some kind of unpleasant jest?'

Her stepmother sniffed and wiped her eyes on a threadbare handkerchief. 'Don't look at me like that, my girl; your father arranged matters with this man before he died. He knew you would never find yourself a husband and that your sisters' debut would be costly. Despite being so beautiful, they will require a sizeable dowry in order to attract the most eligible gentlemen.'

'That's as may be, but I'm at a loss to understand why a complete stranger would be prepared to provide the necessary funds in return for my hand in marriage.'

'Verity, I cannot see why you are so

1

upset. By marrying Sir Ralph Elrick, you will be elevated to the aristocracy, and live in comfort and luxury. If you were in love with another gentleman, then I could see that you might object to an arranged marriage — but you've received not a single offer and you are now at your last prayers. Surely you wish to have a home and children of your own — so why not accept this generous proposal? By so doing, you will ensure that your sisters will find satisfactory partners.'

'I've never met this gentleman, know nothing about him or his home, and yet you think it perfectly in order for me to travel to the wilds of Northumbria and marry him!' She was tempted to throw the offensive letter into the fire, but instead she folded it and handed it back. This was not the dark ages, where brides were bartered in exchange for monetary gain. She had no intention of sacrificing herself so her spoilt sisters could replenish their wardrobes and deck themselves out in silken finery in order to attend fashionable soirées in London.

'I'm going to the library to write a reply. I'm sorry, Mama, but I won't marry this man under any circumstances. I'm sure Papa never agreed to any such thing.'

She left her stepmother sniffing and blowing her nose in the drawing room, and scurried through the freezing corridors to the library. This was her favourite room, and here a fire was always kept burning during the winter months so she could retreat when her parent and siblings became too much to bear.

Sofia and Serena were twins, and naturally her stepmother's favourites. Her sisters had golden curls, bright blue eyes and perfect figures. They had grown up believing they were the centre of the universe and that their older half-sister, who possessed none of their attractive attributes, was solely there to take care of them. Now they were approaching their eighteenth birthday, they would expect to move into society and find themselves rich and adoring husbands in the coming Season. Indeed, she sometimes felt Papa had abandoned his tenuous hold on life deliberately in order to go to a place where he would not be harried morning to night by his extravagant and demanding wife and daughters.

Once in the sanctuary of the library, she closed the door and hurried over to the desk. The sooner this letter was written and sent, the better. She barely had time to find paper and trim her pen before there was a sharp knock on the door. Unused to being disturbed in here, she had no wish for anyone to enter and spoil her peace.

With a sigh of resignation she stood up and crossed the room. To her surprise, Stevens, the ancient butler and the only male member of staff still in their employment, handed her a letter and then tottered off without speaking.

Verity took the missive back to the desk and broke the wax seal. How could this be? She recognised the spidery writing immediately — it was from her father — but he had been dead these past three years.

My dearest Verity,

You will now have received a letter requesting your hand in marriage from Sir Ralph and will no doubt be sitting at your desk in the library about to pen a curt refusal.

Please do not be too hasty — let me explain how this situation has come about. Before I returned from the war a broken man, I had the good fortune to save the life of Sir Ralph, at the cost of my own health. He wanted to know what he could do to repay me and this is what I asked him.

If by the time you were one and twenty he is still a bachelor and you a spinster then he must make you an offer. Elrick is a gentleman with a large fortune and will make you an excellent husband.

Think about it, dearest girl, the

chances of you finding yourself a suitable husband now that your siblings are grown is unlikely. You deserve to be happy, to have a family of your own, and be appreciated in a way that will never take place whilst you remain at home.

By accepting this offer you can leave your selfish sisters and demanding stepmother to their own devices and need never see them again. I can go to meet my maker knowing that my beloved daughter can leave Sanderson Manor and find happiness elsewhere.

I repeat, Elrick will make you an excellent husband, I would not have made this bargain otherwise.

Think of me when you are happy as Lady Elrick living in your castle in Northumbria.

Your loving father

Tears trickled unheeded down her cheeks and she clutched the precious letter to her bosom. This had been Papa's dying wish, and she could not now refuse. She read the letter again and wished that her father had given more details about the appearance and character of the man who was to be her husband.

Her hands were shaking, and she took several steadying breaths in the hope she could restore her composure before writing an acceptance letter to Sir Ralph. The Sanderson family were landed gentry, had an aristocrat or two in their family tree, but were not members of the *ton*. Her own mother had died giving birth to her, and her father had remarried in order to provide his baby daughter with a maternal figure. Being a military man, he was away more than he was at home, and had no wish to leave her to be brought up by servants.

On his brief visits home he had seen a well-run house, three apparently happy children, and a wife who went out of her way to please him. Only when he was grievously injured and forced to return permanently did he fully understand the true situation; but by then, the damage had been done. His coffers were all but empty, his younger daughters quite ruined, and his eldest become withdrawn.

This extraordinary arrangement had been his way of making amends. She would write a letter to her future husband accepting his offer . . . but with one major stipulation. Although eventually she did wish to have children, until she had got to know the man who would be entitled to share her body and her bed, she had no wish for intimacy of any sort.

She sanded the letter, folded it neatly, and sealed it with a blob of red wax. Sending it by express would be extravagant, but now she had made her decision to go, she wanted it arranged as soon as possible.

* * *

Ralph dropped his head into his hands, and sat like that for several minutes until he could bring himself to open the letter that had arrived so promptly from Verity Sanderson. If she had refused — and what sensible young woman would agree to such a bizarre suggestion? — he didn't know if he could face any more lonely months rattling around in this godforsaken castle.

Devil take it! He was made of sterner stuff than this — he'd been given a second chance at life by Colonel Sanderson when dozens of his friends hadn't been so lucky. In the intervening years, he'd put the arrangement to the back of his mind, and concentrated on improving the lot of his tenants, investing his considerable wealth in a variety of enterprises, and trying to make the castle more hospitable. In this last endeavour he'd failed miserably, and this vast grey stone building with its turrets and crenellations still remained an unpleasant place to live. Only by paying extortionate wages to his staff could he keep them there. God knew what the pampered daughter of the colonel would make of it — if she came.

He straightened and broke the seal. He rubbed his eyes, unable for a moment to take in the contents. Verity had agreed to his preposterous proposal, and her only stipulation was that it remained unconsummated until she had got to know him better.

With a wry smile he limped across to the escritoire to pen his reply. He agreed the marriage would be in name only until she chose to make it otherwise — although once she met him, he doubted that day would ever come. It was so damnably far to Hertfordshire he couldn't make that journey himself, or he would go and fetch his future wife.

However, he would send his new travelling carriage and arrange for overnight accommodation to be waiting at each of the posting inns on the journey. He calculated that she would be obliged to make three stops, possibly four if the weather was inclement and made the roads difficult, and the best rooms would be at her disposal.

Presumably she would bring her own

maid; she could hardly travel that distance unaccompanied. There would be ample room for two passengers and their baggage without the necessity of sending a second vehicle.

He had already obtained a special licence, and the wedding could take place as soon as she arrived and the local vicar could perform it in the family chapel. He gave his instructions, knowing they would be followed to the letter, and then summoned the housekeeper and butler. In future they would take their orders from Verity — and damn glad he would be to hand over that tiresome responsibility.

He occupied only a fraction of Castle Elrick, but even so this meant more than two dozen chambers to make ready, and Cook must replenish the larders. It would soon be Christmas and he wanted this celebration to be memorable for his new bride.

Hodgson, the butler, stood silently beside Saxton, the housekeeper, whilst he gave them their instructions. Saxton curtsied and he gestured for her to speak.

'Sir, it's already the middle of December, and the festive season will be upon us very soon. Do you intend to entertain so that you may introduce Lady Elrick to your neighbours?'

'I don't entertain, Saxton. However, if my wife wishes to decorate the house with ribbons and evergreens and invite the neighbours, then she may do so. I suggest you get that organised before the snow sets in. You must ensure that we have sufficient food and drink to cover any eventuality. I wish fires to be lit everywhere, and her ladyship's apartments to be furnished with the best you can find and scrubbed from top to bottom.'

He waved his dismissal and they vanished to carry out his bidding. When he'd inherited the title, his family had been residing in the more convenient and convivial Gloucestershire estate, and the castle had been left to decay in solitary splendour for decades.

Ralph had had no intention of living in so public a place, so had left his mother and grandmother at Elrick Court and made his home where the family had originated. In the three years since he'd been here, a fraction of the building had been restored, but the remainder was still more or less derelict. No one ventured into the turrets or dared walk on the battlements.

His arrival at Castle Elrick had given gainful employment to dozens of families in the neighbourhood, and the pinched, sullen faces of the village folk had been replaced by plump, smiling ones. They were happy to work in his fields, stables or gardens, but reluctant to come through the doors. When he'd enquired as to why, Hodgson had muttered some nonsense about ghosts and evil spirits. Ralph, though, had no time for silly superstition, and knew the strange noises he heard were no more than the usual sounds one would expect to hear in an ancient building.

Although five miles from the nearest

large house, his neighbours had still taken the trouble to call in order to introduce themselves, but he had refused to see any of them. After a while, the invitations to attend various routs and parties had ceased to arrive, and they left him to his own devices. This was how he preferred things to be — but when Verity arrived, she would want to mingle with her peers, which no doubt would mean morning calls and evening parties. However, as long as he was not required to participate, she could do as she pleased.

He wanted her to be happy here, would make every effort to be the best husband he was capable of being . . . but he thought the enterprise was doomed to failure, and that within a few months he would once more be mouldering in this decaying edifice by himself.

By marrying Verity, he would be fulfilling his promise to the brave man who had saved him from a gruesome death at the cost of his own good health. Even if she abandoned him — and he wouldn't blame her if she did — she would depart a wealthy woman, and be able to set herself up anywhere in the country to live in style. Eventually, it might even be possible to obtain an annulment so she could marry again; though when he'd asked his lawyer, he'd been told it was a complicated procedure and required an act of Parliament.

In less than a week his bride would arrive — and, God willing, would still agree to marry him once they had met.

* * *

Four days after sending her response, a handsome travelling carriage turned into the drive, and Verity realised this had been sent instead of a reply to her letter.

'Sally, how close are we to being ready to depart?' She checked the overmantel clock and saw the time was just after eleven.

Her abigail pointed to the open

15

trunks in the sitting room. 'Almost done, miss; I reckon we could leave in half an hour. The trunk with your books and painting and writing things is already strapped and downstairs. I've just the last items to put into these, and I'm done.'

'I shall check that Fred and Billy are also ready to go. Kindly put out my travelling ensemble: I'll be back directly to change.'

Her stepmother and half-sisters had gone to visit friends, and wouldn't be back until the evening. They would be relieved to see her go, so there was no necessity to remain until they returned. Verity hurried out to the stables to see that her only valuable possession, her stallion Black Star, was ready for the long journey.

Fred greeted her warmly. 'We're ready to go, Miss Sanderson. Shall we wait and follow the coach, or make our own way? We'll need to take it slowly, I reckon you'll have fresh horses every time you stop.'

'As long as you arrive safely, I don't mind how long you take. I neglected to enquire as to the size and state of Sir Ralph's stables — but he's a wealthy man, so I would be surprised if he didn't have ample room for the three animals I'm bringing with me.'

'Sinbad and Sultan have just got back from the blacksmith, our saddlebags are packed, and we've more than enough blunt to pay for our accommodation and food.'

'All three will need rugs, for they are not used to the temperatures we will find in Northumbria.'

She paused to stroke the massive head of her horse before hurrying back to the house. The front door was open and footmen were carrying out the trunks to the waiting vehicle.

A smartly dressed coachman bowed and then touched his beaver with the tip of his whip. 'Good morning, Miss Sanderson. I'm Jim Roberts, coachman to Sir Ralph. Will you be ready to leave as soon as your luggage is stowed?'

She nodded. 'I shall be ready in a quarter of an hour. Will the team be sufficiently rested to depart then?'

'We picked them up less than an hour ago; they're strong beasts, and will do until we make our first stop for refreshments.'

★ ★ ★

Verity didn't look back as the carriage rumbled down the drive. Sanderson Manor had never been a happy place for her, and she had no regrets about leaving. There had been no opportunity to travel, and she was eagerly anticipating seeing new places and meeting new people.

Sir Ralph had provided every luxury for the journey, and Verity enjoyed every moment of the three days. The weather remained cold and dry, and they made excellent time. As they approached the neighbourhood in which her new home was situated, she was struck by the bleak beauty of the moorland, the lack of trees and the hilly nature of the countryside. Sally had been gazing out of the window too.

'We've not passed many villages or towns, miss. I'd no idea we were coming to such a remote part of the country.'

'It's very beautiful, don't you think? I'm sure we will settle in well — but remember, I promised that if you cannot like it, then you may return to Sanderson Manor.'

'No thank you, miss, I'd rather be up here with you than back there with them.' Sally shivered and pulled the rug more firmly around her knees. 'It's much colder here; you're going to need some warmer cloaks and thicker gowns if you're not to freeze.'

The carriage settled into a companionable silence until the glint of water caught Verity's eye. She swivelled in her seat and pushed her nose against the glass like a small child. 'Look, Sally, it's the sea. Isn't it spectacular? I'd no idea we'd be living by the coast.'

As she spoke the coach rocked to a standstill and a smiling face appeared upside down at the window. Quickly Sally undid the strap and lowered the glass so the dangling coachman could speak to them.

'You can see Castle Elrick just ahead — it overlooks the sea. We'll be there in half an hour. The master will have seen us and be waiting to greet you.'

The biting wind that had whistled through the open window had chilled her to the marrow. She was relieved when her maid fumbled it shut. The horses, sensing they were close to their warm stables, increased their pace, so the carriage was racing towards her destination.

It slowed to negotiate the walled entrance and then unhurriedly circled a large enclosure and halted at the massive, iron-studded front door. Only then did it occur to Verity that one might have expected an eager bridegroom to ride out and greet his prospective bride, not remain inside in the warm.

2

Four footmen flanked the impressive door and they bounded forward as soon as the carriage rolled to a stop. There was still no sign of her prospective husband, and this omission was beginning to bother Verity. The two people waiting at the head of the stone steps must be the butler and housekeeper; they both moved down to meet her as soon as the carriage door was opened.

Ignoring the hand held out to assist her, she waited for the servants to introduce themselves.

'Welcome to Castle Elrick, Miss Sanderson. I am Hodgson, butler here, and this is Saxton, the housekeeper. We are entirely at your service. Anything that you require, you only have to ask.'

He bowed and the housekeeper curtsied, then they stood aside so she could make her way to the front door.

As soon as she'd exited the carriage, her heart had plummeted to her boots. Everywhere she looked, she was surrounded by tall stone walls. The castle was a forbidding place, not at all the romantic building she'd imagined.

An icy wind whipped her cloak around her ankles and her cheeks were already numb. Perhaps being so close to a northern sea was not going to be as enjoyable as she'd thought. Where was her future husband?

'Is Sir Ralph indisposed?' The couple exchanged glances and her doubts about her decision to come multiplied tenfold.

'The master is waiting in the blue drawing room, Miss Sanderson. However, he thought you might wish to visit your apartment before you met.' Hodgson didn't smile; in fact, he was a miserable sort of fellow.

The butler's meaning was quite clear. She was expected to repair her appearance before daring to approach the man she was going to marry. 'How thoughtful of him, but I wish to see him immediately.' She stepped round the two of them, ignoring their shocked expressions, and marched straight into what might be her future home.

Sally was with her. 'Here, miss, let me take your cloak and bonnet. You look perfectly fine — don't take any notice of those two.'

Verity had come in so swiftly the housekeeper and butler were still a few paces behind, but a nervous footman was lurking in a corner. 'Conduct me to Sir Ralph immediately.'

He could hardly refuse a direct command, and she was taken down a surprisingly warm flagstone passageway until he stopped in front of an enormous arched doorway. He didn't announce her arrival, just pointed and hurried away, leaving them alone.

As the door was open, she could hardly knock. 'I shall go in, Sally, but you must stay with me at all times.'

Her heart was hammering so loudly she thought she would be unable to hear anything else. There was only one reason why he could be hiding from her: he must be so severely disfigured he feared her reaction. There was no other way of accounting for his behaviour. This would also explain why an eligible bachelor should be obliged to obtain a wife in this way.

Her anger at his incivility faded, but it was replaced by a fear that she wouldn't be able to disguise her horror or bring herself to marry such a man as this.

The chamber was as depressing as the rest of the castle, but at least it was warm. There was little light coming in through the mullioned windows and no candles had been lit. This merely confirmed her suspicions. This gentleman was to be pitied, not blamed or rejected. Papa had selected him for her and she would abide by his decision, however difficult it might prove to be.

She walked slowly into the room, scanning the space for a glimpse of Sir Ralph. Had she been brought to the wrong place? No — the walls were blue so this must be the blue drawing room.

Then a slight movement on her left caught her attention. Immediately she dropped into a deep curtsy. 'Sir Ralph, I am Verity Sanderson.'

'I should hope that you are, and I am Ralph Elrick, at your service.' His voice came from beside her, and so startled her that she almost lost her balance. His hand caught her elbow and steadied her. 'That, my dear, is the last time you will curtsy to me.'

His voice was deep and attractive, his grip strong — perhaps she would risk a glance at him. Nervously, she raised her head, expecting to be horrified by what she saw. She spoke without thinking.

'Sir Ralph, why do you hide away? I expected you to be . . . ' Her voice trailed away in embarrassment.

He was still holding her hand and his chuckle was as warm and rich as his voice. 'Come, Verity, I shall stand by the window so you can examine me more closely.'

He led her across the vast expanse of expensive Brussels carpet, and she noticed that he limped, but not so much as to make him ungainly. Her cheeks were burning and she wished she could run away and hide after her appalling rudeness.

'Now, what do you think? Will I do, or are you going to run away?'

The scar that marred his face ran from under his hair, across his left eye, and disappeared under his chin. He was fortunate not to have lost the sight in that eye. Without conscious thought she reached out and ran her finger along the puckered skin. 'I'm glad that my father saved your life, and I've no intention of going anywhere.'

His hand trapped hers against his cheek for a second, and then he released her and moved away. 'You are a sensible young lady, and I apologise profusely for not having the courage to greet you outside. I hope you had a comfortable journey.' He gestured towards a group of sagging armchairs and sofas grouped around a roaring fire. 'Shall we sit down?'

At this point he noticed Sally was still with them, and flicked his fingers at her. Her maid curtsied and backed out as if in the presence of royalty, leaving them alone.

'If this arrangement is to be successful, we must be honest with each other. You must always tell me what you're feeling, and I shall do the same.'

'In which case, I must tell you that my first impressions of Castle Elrick are not favourable. Although it is considerably warmer than Sanderson Manor, I find it gloomy and oppressive.'

He looked less than pleased at her frankness, but he had asked her to be honest, so could not cavil. 'What did you expect? This building is ancient, hundreds of years old: it was built by my ancestors to protect their lands from invasion.'

'I know nothing of castles or of Northumbria. I apologise for criticising your home. No doubt I'll come to appreciate it in time.' She didn't sit, but continued towards the door. 'If you'll excuse me, Sir Ralph, I wish to go to my apartment. Would you be kind enough to ring for a footman to conduct me there?'

He viewed her through narrowed eyes for a second and then nodded. 'There will be someone outside the door. No doubt it will take you a day or two to get your bearings. Dinner is served at five o'clock. There is no need to change.' His hand flicked for a second time in the same casual gesture of dismissal he'd given to her maid, and then he turned his back on her.

For a second, she was tempted to give him a severe set-down, but rapidly reconsidered. He was a formidable size and not a gentleman to be trifled with.

Sally was waiting outside and had obviously been in conversation with the footman.

'I wish to go to my rooms. Have refreshments sent up immediately.' She addressed these remarks to the servant and he bowed. However, his reply was incomprehensible as his accent was so thick. She presumed he'd just been agreeing.

This time, she took more notice of her surroundings, but didn't revise her opinion. The place was grey and depressing. However, it was also clean and warm. She stopped to gaze at the two suits of armour that stood guard on either side of the massive front door. There were countless shields, swords and other ancient weapons hanging from the walls, which did nothing to improve her original decision to dislike the place.

The stone staircase hugged the wall and was surprisingly narrow for such a place. She could only suppose that it had been built in this way so that the upstairs floor could be protected more easily from invaders — should they manage to get over the drawbridge, under the portcullis, and through the door.

She was happy with her accommodation — it was commodious, clean, and pleasantly warm. However, even with thick tapestries hanging against all the walls, the rooms were still unfriendly; but she supposed she would get used to them in time.

No sooner had they stepped into the sitting room than two maids, so similar in appearance they must be siblings, shuffled in from the bedroom. They curtsied and mumbled something unintelligible. Sally took charge. 'Come along then, we must unpack the trunks and prepare a nice warm bath for Miss Sanderson.'

The three of them vanished, leaving Verity to wander around the chamber examining everything that had been provided for her. There was a pretty escritoire, three side tables, and another larger one, presumably for eating. The curtains had been freshly laundered and all the upholstery was spotless; but none of the furniture was new, and all of it was made from old-fashioned oak.

The thickness of the castle walls meant there was ample room for a seat beneath each window, but unless she stood on this she couldn't see out. Having the windows so high in the walls must be another safety feature, but it made the room dark and oppressive even with two fires and a dozen candles burning.

One section of the wall was given over to bookshelves, and she went to examine the titles stored there. None of them were of much interest to her: they were all on flora and fauna, religious tracts or literary essays — there were no novels of any sort. She hoped she would never become so bored she would be obliged to dip into them.

A short while later, yet another young girl staggered in with a laden tray. She was certainly not going to go hungry whilst living here. She thanked the girl and sent her away as she had no wish to be waited on or watched whilst she ate.

As she was munching through the delicious repast she had ample time to consider her situation. Sir Ralph was disfigured but not disastrously so; indeed, without his scars he would have been impossibly handsome. She closed her eyes and let his image drift into her head. He must be at least two yards tall, with broad shoulders and a deep chest. His teeth were all his own and, as far as she had seen, were healthy and white. His hair was as black as her stallion's coat and his eyes a strange blue-grey. Despite his limp he appeared strong and healthy.

Her lips curved in an involuntary smile. Her review of her prospective husband was of the same sort that she would give to a horse she intended to purchase. Was he disappointed with his bargain and regretting having sent for her?

When she had finished her meal, Sally came in to say that hot water for her bath would not be ready for another hour or so.

'No matter, I shall spend time looking around the castle. As you are busy unpacking, I shall go with the footman who is waiting outside the door.'

'You don't want to be going on the battlements, miss, they don't look safe.'

'I've no intention of doing so, I shall

leave that until the weather is more clement. Although Sir Ralph said there was no need to change for dinner, I want to look smart, so could you find and press something suitable?'

The thought of taking a bath on her return to her apartment was a pleasant one, but she decided she would make the most of this opportunity as she had no intention of asking the unfortunate kitchen maids to trudge up and down stairs more often than was necessary. In future she would complete her ablutions with a jug and basin, and restrict her bathing to special occasions.

An unexpected warmth travelled from top to toe at the thought of what might be considered a special occasion which would make total immersion in warm water essential. Sir Ralph — he would be Ralph to her in future — although not perfect, was a very attractive gentleman, and she thought it wouldn't be long before he charmed her into his bed.

The young man who had been

designated her guide appeared the instant she opened the sitting room door. 'I wish you to show me around the castle — obviously only the occupied portion — not the rest.'

He nodded and smiled, and this time she was almost sure he said he would be pleased to take her anywhere she wished. Hopefully her ears would soon become attuned to this Northumbrian accent and she would be able to follow everything that was said to her.

Castle Elrick had been built long ago, but had been updated over the centuries, and extra fireplaces and chimneys installed. There was nothing that could be done about the high, narrow windows or the damp, cold, stone walls, however.

After an hour of looking into dreary, old-fashioned rooms, she was ready to return. Then she noticed a door tucked away in the corner of the passage. 'Where does this lead? I didn't know there were attics here.'

The young man shook his head. He

wasn't unintelligent, and this time he spoke more slowly and enunciated each syllable as if speaking to a small child. 'Don't go through there, miss, it's not safe.'

Presumably it led to the roof, and she had no wish to creep about outside. 'Very well, I think I've seen enough for today. Please take me back to my apartment.'

Her bath was ready when she returned. As she stepped into the warm, scented water, she became aware that Sally was upset about something. 'What is it? Please tell me, I don't want you to be unhappy here.'

'Kirsty, one of the girls helping up here, says that Morag, a scullery maid, was sent to fetch vegetables from the cold store and never came back.'

★ ★ ★

Ralph waited until he heard the door close before he turned. He'd asked her to be honest and then, when she'd been so, he'd taken umbrage and got on his high horse. She was right to criticise Castle Elrick — it was a monstrous place and if he had a choice he might consider residing elsewhere.

Verity was not what he'd been expecting, and without doubt he'd got by far the best of the bargain. She was above average height, well-rounded, and although not what he would call a beauty, she was a damn sight better-looking than he was. Her hair was nut-brown, and her eyes . . . damn it to hell — what colour were her eyes? He smiled ruefully. One might say they were Beauty and the Beast.

He'd been so taken aback by her lack of disgust at his hideous face, and by the fact that she'd actually reached out and touched his scar, he'd scarcely noticed anything else. He had no mirrors in the castle, apart from the one he'd bought especially for Verity's chambers. Had his appearance improved since he'd left Elrick Court? The looks — first of horror, then of pity — he'd seen on his mother's and grandmother's faces were forever etched on his memory. They had been enough to send him away, to make him set up his home in the deserted wilds of Northumbria.

He'd been fêted all his life, admired by every lady he met, had known himself to be a handsome man. He'd had every expectation of being able to select his bride from the cream of the debutantes when he eventually decided to set up his nursery. Now he was to marry an unsuitable girl in order to fulfil a promise to an old comrade.

Verity would not settle here. She was too outspoken and headstrong and would find the isolation difficult. He hadn't had much contact with the Almighty since his return from the Peninsula: after what he'd experienced and seen, his faith had been sorely tested. He threw himself into a chair and gazed into the fire, letting his thoughts drift heavenwards.

After a few minutes he was able to view the situation more calmly. He realised he would be a fool not to do everything in his power to keep Verity happy, and convince her that, despite his obvious drawbacks, he would make her a good husband.

Although he had thought he wanted a quiet, submissive girl for his wife, he now knew this wasn't the truth. Being married to someone like that would be dull — being married to an intelligent, argumentative young lady like Verity would enliven his boring existence.

He sighed and put his hands behind his head, stretching out his booted legs towards the flames. He'd lived the life of a monk since returning to England, and the thought of wooing Verity into bed sent a surge of excitement around his body. Then reality replaced his elation.

Who was he fooling? She might have accepted the scars on his face; however, when she saw him unclothed, she would be revolted. His right leg was hideous, and he was lucky to still have it attached to his body. Not to mention the marks that ran up his left side . . .

He must have dozed off, as the next thing he knew, Hodgson was by his chair.

'Sir Ralph, you must come at once. Morag, the scullery maid, has disappeared.'

3

Ralph surged to his feet, instantly alert; his years of serving as a soldier had given him that ability. 'How long has she been missing?'

Hodgson shook his head. 'I'm not exactly sure, sir, but half an hour at least. Cook sent two other girls out to look, but there was no sign of Morag. If we don't find her soon, the kitchen staff will leave. There's been muttering already about the Elrick Ghosts having come back.'

'Why in God's name has this happened now? Any talk of ghosts and ghoulies will send Miss Sanderson back to her family. I'm certain there's a rational explanation — there always is. There's no such thing as supernatural beings.'

He didn't stop to find his greatcoat, muffler or gloves, but ran through the house and straight outside to the vegetable store from where the wretched girl had supposedly vanished. The trouble with being in such a remote place was that the population was overly superstitious — after all, they had little else to occupy themselves with on the long, dark nights of winter.

A group of outside men were hovering nervously outside the door that led down to the cellar in which the vegetables were stored for the winter. Silently, they parted and allowed him through, but none of them offered to accompany him down the stairs.

'Has anyone been in to look, or have you been skulking up here?'

Jethro, the head groom, touched his cap. 'We went down, but there's no sign of her, sir. Go and look for yourself.'

This was hardly the sort of response one might expect from a servant, but here in the north, folk didn't hold their employers in such high esteem.

He'd had the foresight to bring a lantern, and held this aloft as he marched straight down the pitch-dark staircase. 'Morag, Morag, are you there?'

His voice echoed hollowly and there was no response. The root cellar was not that big; however, it led into further storerooms, and he was certain none of the men would have ventured any further than they had to.

After checking that the girl wasn't lying injured anywhere behind the sacks and boxes, he headed for the narrow doorway at the rear of the storeroom. Why she should have gone through there, he'd no idea; but people didn't vanish into thin air, so she must be somewhere, lost in the maze of cellars and passageways that ran under the castle.

He ducked through the doorway and continued to call as he made his way slowly onwards, stopping to look into each cellar as he passed. After a few minutes he came to a junction — if he ventured much further, he might well become lost himself.

He retraced his steps and emerged blinking into the courtyard. 'I need a piece of chalk; I don't want to go astray down there.'

Minutes later he retraced his steps, and this time he marked the wall with a cross so he could find his way back. He took the left-hand turning and continued to call and search, but after fifteen minutes decided the girl could not have got any further in the time.

His lantern sent flickering shadows in all directions, and despite his certainty that the child's disappearance was no more than an accident, his hands were unpleasantly clammy. He made his way as quickly as he could to the junction, and this time took the right-hand passageway. 'Morag, Morag, answer me if you can.'

A faint moan from just ahead made the hairs on the back of his neck prickle. He lowered the lantern and, sure enough, huddled against the wall was the missing maid. He dropped to his knees beside her.

'Morag, little one, are you hurt?' He quickly ran his hands over her shivering body and could find no obvious injuries. The girl was little more than a child; small wonder that she'd become disorientated down here. She must have dropped her candle and become lost. Cook should have sent someone older, or at least given her a companion.

'Put your arm around my neck. I'll carry you back.'

Her little arm slipped around his neck, and he put his left arm under her body and transferred the lantern to that hand. Then he put his right arm under her knees and hoisted her into the air. Her skirts were wet — the poor child had emptied her bladder.

She weighed nothing at all, and even a man such as himself was able to carry her and make his way to the surface without difficulty. As soon as he appeared, the atmosphere changed. 'Take her in to Cook, Jethro; she must have dropped her candle and wandered off in the dark.'

He handed his burden over and

made his way to the front door. He hadn't intended to change for dinner, but had no choice, for he could hardly appear as he was. He would have words with the housekeeper later, and make sure she told Cook to take better care of her maids in future.

His valet was more a friend than a servant, as he had been with him throughout his campaign in Spain and Portugal. Ralph could speak to him freely and know nothing he said would be repeated downstairs in the servants' hall. Jenkins was from London, and even after three years here still found the locals strange. Fortunately, four other men from Elrick Court had agreed to accompany Ralph in his self-imposed banishment, so Jenkins had others of his ilk to fraternise with.

'I've everything waiting for you, sir — I reckoned you'd need a bit of a spit and polish after creeping around them cellars for half an hour. Found the little girl, did you?'

'I certainly did. She must have

dropped her candle and then got lost in the dark — nothing to do with the supernatural.'

Ralph shrugged off his jacket and waistcoat, but then saw that the damp patch from carrying Morag had reached his shirt, so that must come off as well. As always, he carefully avoided glancing down at his disfigurement. He washed his face and hands, then held out his arms for Jenkins to slip on a fresh shirt.

'I've put out a right smart silk waistcoat for you; reckon you'll want to look your best tonight, won't you, sir?'

'I've not really thought about it, Jenkins, but I suppose I should make an effort. I told Miss Sanderson not to dress, but no doubt she will do so anyway.'

As soon as his stock was tied to his satisfaction, Ralph put on a fresh jacket. His unmentionables had been sponged clean, and his Hessians were once more fit to be seen. 'Will I pass muster, Jenkins?'

'Very good, sir, and I'm sure your

young lady will be impressed. I sent word to the reverend gentleman to be here at ten o'clock tomorrow morning.'

'God's teeth! So soon?' His man raised a bushy eyebrow and Ralph smiled. 'You're right; the sooner the knot's tied, the better. Her reputation will be in tatters if she remains here unchaperoned for more than one night.'

'I thought as you might like to be wed in your dress uniform, Sir Ralph? A young lady always likes a man in uniform.'

'As I never actually resigned my commission, I suppose I am entitled to wear it. Doing so will bring back unpleasant memories, but I'll be guided by your superior knowledge of such things.'

Jenkins chuckled and brushed a piece of invisible fluff from his master's jacket. 'Will you be late retiring, sir?'

'I shouldn't think so. I wish I could remove my boots by myself, then you could have the evenings free.'

His manservant shrugged. 'I spend

my time downstairs and have little to do as it is. Could do with a bit more; after soldiering, living here ain't too exciting.'

Ralph slapped him on the back. 'Quiet is good, my friend, but I promise I'll find you something more invigorating to do in future. In fact, why don't you talk to Morag and make sure my interpretation of events is correct? Then investigate the cellars yourself so we may put paid to any more nonsense about ghosts.'

'The winter solstice will be here soon, and that's always a time for outlandish shenanigans and such. It won't take much to set them off again, and then we'll lose a few more men and women. You'd think they would be pleased to have a decent wage and good employment, and not let such silliness upset them.'

Ralph headed for the drawing room, leaving his valet muttering to himself about strange customs and ignorant country folk.

★ ★ ★

Verity, from her position in the centre of the drawing room, watched her future husband limp across the vast hall. He had changed his raiment, not to evening dress, but had on a dark blue jacket, lighter blue waistcoat and immaculate shirt and neckcloth.

She glanced down at her gown and was glad Sally had persuaded her to put on this ensemble. Russet wool suited her, as did the fashionable high waist. Her stepmother had always insisted they put on their finest silks to dine even when they were without guests. Being able to dress for the weather was another thing she liked about the castle etiquette.

'Good evening, sir. Did you know that it's snowing?'

Her smile was friendly, and he responded in kind. 'If it isn't snowing from November to March, it would be more remarkable, Verity.' His use of her given name was quite deliberate, and he was waiting for her to poker up and complain.

'In which case, I shall start again. Good evening, Ralph; how lucky I was to travel here without snow.'

His laughter was quite irresistible and she joined in. 'Would you like a drink before we dine?' He gestured towards an impressive array of decanters on a massive sideboard.

'No thank you, I rarely consume alcohol. I much prefer lemonade, tea or coffee.'

'Then we shall go through to the dining room immediately. I can't abide being fussed over, so my meals are always served in the chafing dishes and I help myself. If you wish to change this, then feel free to do so. From tomorrow, the running of the household will be in your hands.'

He didn't offer his arm and for some reason she was disappointed. They strolled to a door halfway down the room, and she discovered this led directly to a modest chamber which was obviously used to dine in.

His previous comment had been

bothering her. 'I would prefer to get to know the staff and understand how the house is run before I take control.'

'You will be mistress of Castle Elrick when we marry tomorrow morning, and have no choice in the matter.' He said this as if he was discussing the weather, not something so momentous as their nuptials.

'I see. Is the unseemly rush because you fear I might change my mind and return to Hertfordshire?'

'No, not entirely. You are unchaperoned and I've no wish to damage your reputation.'

He had turned away from her so she couldn't see his expression, but his stance was rigid. 'I am happy with my bargain, Ralph; it was my father's dying wish to see me married to you. He wouldn't have arranged things in this way if he didn't think we would be happy together.'

'I sincerely hope that's the case, sweetheart, and I give you my word I'll do everything I can to be a good husband.'

He gestured to the groaning buffet and together they lifted each heavy silver lid to peer at the contents before deciding what to take. She scarcely noticed what she ate, but it was all delicious, far better than anything she'd ever had before.

Whilst they dined, they talked of this and that; and when he asked if she would like the house decorated for Christmas, she was delighted.

'It's no longer fashionable to decorate one's house with evergreens, but I should love to make this place more cheerful . . .' She stopped, horrified that she'd once more criticised his ancestral home.

'Don't look so worried, I agree with you entirely. This is a sullen place, I don't believe anyone who lived here was happy, and the place reflects that lack of joy.'

'Forgive me for asking, but why do you remain here if you dislike it so much?' He looked at her as if she were a simpleton, then she understood. 'If you are hiding away in this dismal place because you fear your appearance will frighten the children, then you are being foolish beyond words. You are no longer an Adonis, but you are still a very handsome man.'

He opened and shut his mouth a few times like a fish floundering on the bank, and his comical expression made her laugh, which did not improve the situation. He slammed his hands down on the table and rose to his feet.

Instinctively, she cowered back into her chair, expecting to be roared at. However, he spoke quietly, and this was infinitely more terrifying. 'You forget your place, madam. I'm master here, and you will not speak to me like that again. Do you understand me?'

Her tongue stuck to the roof of her mouth and she was incapable of answering. His eyes were almost black, and she saw something hard and dark in the man she was to marry the next day. How could she tie herself to someone who might be violent?

Her dinner was threatening to return, and she clapped her hands to her mouth and swallowed, praying she would not disgrace herself in front of him. He had already taken her in dislike, and seeing her cast up her accounts would make the rift wider.

To her astonishment his grim expression vanished. 'Dammit — hold on. I'll find you a receptacle.' In two strides he was at the sideboard, and tipped the contents of one of the chafing dishes into another, then was beside her in seconds. 'Here, use this.' The object was slammed down in front of her, causing her glass of lemonade to spill into her lap. Her nausea was replaced by anger, and now she too was on her feet.

'Look what you've done to my new gown. First you shout at me for no reason, and now this. I don't believe I wish to marry you after all.'

She attempted to step round him, but he remained in her way. His voice was soft, but his words were not. 'You called me 'foolish beyond words' — if anyone else had the temerity to say such a thing, they would live to regret it.'

He was too close, and she could almost feel his body heat pulsing towards her. Her hands moved of their own volition and she shoved him hard in the chest, sending him staggering backwards before his injured leg gave way so he sprawled on the floor.

Her intention had only been to get past, not to cause him to fall. She dropped to her knees beside him. His eyes were closed, and she feared she'd done him serious harm. 'Ralph, speak to me. Shall I call for assistance?'

Still he lay there without opening his eyes, and she was about to scramble to her feet when one hand shot out and grasped her elbow, holding her a prisoner. His eyes opened — he was no more injured than she was. His intense blue-grey stare pinned her like a butterfly to a board.

'Well, Verity, how shall I proceed? What do you suggest is a suitable punishment for pushing your future husband to the floor after having first insulted him?'

She didn't like his expression one little bit. Was he intending to tip her over his knee and spank her? 'I apologise for causing you to fall, but you were in my way.' She was almost sure his grip was loosening. 'I also apologise for calling you foolish — but I did call you handsome as well.'

He jerked her forward and she fell across his chest. Before she could protest, his other arm was about her waist, pinning her down; she tensed, expecting to receive a series of stinging slaps on her *derrière*. Instead, he rolled sideways, taking her with him, so she was now half beneath him and he was above.

Every inch of her was touching him: her breasts were crushed into his jacket and her legs were indecently entangled with his. Then he lowered his head and covered her mouth gently with his own. There was nothing she could do but endure, so she remained rigid, waiting for him to complete his punishment and release her.

His free hand began to stroke her

hair, and his lips travelled from the corner of her mouth to her ear and back, leaving a trail of heat in their wake. Being kissed wasn't as awful as she'd expected — in fact, she was beginning to rather enjoy it.

What would his hair feel like if she touched it? Did she dare? Her fingers were on their way when abruptly he rolled and, in one remarkably smooth move, regained his feet, pulling her up beside him.

'You are a baggage, my love, and I fear you are going to run me ragged once we are wed.' He spun her round and sent her on her way with a painful slap. 'Go to bed before I do something we will both regret.'

She didn't wait for a second warning but gathered her skirts and dashed for the nearest door. She slammed it behind her and ran headlong in what she thought was the direction of the hall. After a few minutes, she realised she was lost. This was a part of the castle she didn't recognise.

Just ahead of her she saw the entrance to a second staircase and ran towards it. This could only lead in one direction — that of the first floor where she would find her apartment. She was only on the fifth step when she realised she needed a candle and turned back, but as she did so, the light from the wall sconces in the passageway below went out and she missed her step. As she tumbled forwards, she cried out and thought she heard voices — then everything went black.

4

Ralph watched Verity run away, and for the first time since his return from war felt that life might possibly be worth living. He was about to help himself to further food when he realised she'd taken the door that led into a little-used passageway and might well become lost.

Cursing under his breath at his stupidity in not stopping her, he hurried to the exit she'd taken and stood for a moment, undecided in which direction to search. To the left would eventually lead to the servants' quarters; to the right was a part of the castle not yet restored.

There was no danger involved if she ended up with his staff, but she could get into difficulty if she went the other way. He decided it made sense to go towards the derelict part of the building. He turned around the second corner and a strange chill flickered down his spine. The next moment, the wall sconces were snuffed out as if by an invisible hand, and he heard Verity call out.

His instinct was to race towards her cry, but he remained still until his eyes adjusted to the darkness and he could see sufficiently to head in the right direction. Where the devil was she? After that one shout there'd been nothing further, and the corridor in front of him was deserted.

Then he spotted a door he didn't recall having seen before. As he watched, it seemed to shift before his eyes. He'd never moved so fast in his life — he snatched it open to discover her slumped in a heap just inside. In one deft movement he scooped her up and fell backwards out of the doorway; as he crashed to the flagstones with her in his arms, the door seemed to disappear.

He blinked, not believing what he'd

just seen. He'd cushioned her fall with his body and cracked the back of his head on the flagstones when he landed. Was this what had caused him to imagine that a door had just vanished?

Verity stirred in his arms, and he knew he had to make an effort to pull himself together, ignoring the pain in the back of his head and the fact that his vision was blurred. He was a military man, and had suffered far worse than this and continued to fight.

Then she shifted and her warm weight sent shock waves of heat to his nether regions. This jerked him into action as he had no wish to cause either of them embarrassment. 'Sweetheart, I'm going to put you on the floor. Don't try and get up for a moment — not until I'm sure you're unhurt.'

Her eyes flickered open and she stared at him in bewilderment. Then her eyes widened in horror. 'Ralph, there's blood soaking into your neckcloth. Quickly, let me take a look.'

Verity moved herself from his lap and

examined the back of his head. 'I must stop the bleeding, and I'm sure that you'll need sutures in the wound.' She flicked back her skirt and tore two long strips from her petticoat.

He wanted to tell her not to worry, to ask her what had happened, but his mouth was stuffed with cotton and his eyes refused to stay open.

* * *

Verity knew a little about head wounds, having dealt with one of her half-sisters when she'd tumbled down the stairs a year or so ago. The physician had told her that they bled profusely, but that as long as the blood was stemmed, the patient usually made a full and rapid recovery.

When she had folded one strip of cloth into a pad, she placed it against the gash, and then speedily bound the other makeshift bandage around his head in order to hold it in place. Satisfied she'd done all she could, she gently placed his head onto the flagstones and stood up.

There was something strange about this passageway, and for a moment she couldn't think what it was. Then she remembered that the sconces had gone out — but, strangely, they were now alight again.

She shivered. There was something eerie about this place, and the sooner she and Ralph were in the occupied part of the castle, the happier she'd be.

She wasn't sure if she should leave him and go in search of help, or sit with his head in her lap and shout until someone came. She would try shouting first. Her legs were unsteady and she ached from head to foot as if she'd taken a tumble from her horse.

She yelled at the top of her voice. After her second shout, she was rewarded by the sound of pounding footsteps approaching from the left, and a group of men rushed around the corner. They were led by a burly individual with flame-red hair who skidded to a halt beside her.

'Sir Ralph cracked his head when he fell backwards — I've stopped the bleeding, but he has lapsed into unconsciousness. I think he will need sutures in the gash, and a physician must be sent for immediately.'

'Jenkins, the master's valet, at your service, miss. I'll take care of him now. I've stitched him up a number of times and can do so again without sending for the doctor. You go to your apartment and get yourself warm, and I'll send for you when he's recovered his senses.'

'I would do so, Jenkins, if I had any idea in which direction to go.'

He snapped his fingers and one of the footmen who had accompanied him jumped to attention and bowed in her direction. He said, or at least she thought he said, 'If you would care to follow me, Miss Sanderson, I'll show you the way.'

Verity was reluctant to leave Ralph, but his manservant seemed competent, and there was little else she could do.

She was about to go when she stopped and stared at the wall. She blinked and looked again. The door through which she'd gone was there once more.

'Where does that door lead to?'

Jenkins looked and frowned. 'I've no idea, miss; can't say that I've noticed it before.'

As she followed the footman down the identical passageways, she reviewed the extraordinary events of the past half an hour. A door that came and went? Ghostly voices? Was the castle haunted, or was she losing her senses? Then something else occurred to her that was equally unexpected.

She had been dismissed by a servant and she'd followed his instructions without demure. Everything was topsy-turvy here, but at least her life was no longer tedious. Indeed, in the past few hours there had been more excitement and adventure than she'd so far experienced in her entire existence.

'Thank you, I'm familiar with my sur-roundings now, and can find my own way. Tell me, is it usual for so many members of staff to be on duty?'

'Yes, miss, Mr Hodgson likes us all to be around until the master has retired.'

Verity glanced at the clock on the mantelpiece and was shocked to find the time was only eight o'clock — far too early to go to bed. Sally had been busy: the empty bookshelves were now half-filled with volumes, and her painting equipment was neatly stacked below them.

She selected a book at random and took it to an armchair positioned close to the cheerful fire. But the story failed to hold her attention, and after an hour she tossed it aside. Tomorrow she would be mistress of this establishment, and she refused to be given orders by a minion in future. She would see how her husband-to-be was progressing for herself.

Ralph's apartment was adjacent to hers and there was a communicating door from her bedchamber to his. She had made sure the bolt was across on her side, and it was possible he had done the same. However, the door opened smoothly once she had unlocked it, and she stepped into his room and looked around with interest. It was twice the size of hers, dominated by a massive tester bed which required a set of wooden steps to climb onto it.

It was impossible to see the rest of the chamber as the only illumination came from a large fire. As there was no one sitting with him, presumably the patient had been stitched up and left to sleep, so her visit was unnecessary.

'Come in, sweetheart; an unexpected but welcome visit.' He sounded remarkably well for a gentleman who had been bleeding so profusely an hour or so ago.

She was tempted to retreat, but decided to see for herself that he was fully recovered. 'May I come in? I've no wish to intrude.'

'Please do. We need to talk about what happened this evening, and I think it best if we do so without being overheard. The servants are already spooked, and further evidence that this place is haunted will mean they might well leave en masse.'

There was a chair positioned by the fire that would do very well. She had no intention of approaching the bed; he'd already overstepped the mark once tonight, and she wouldn't put it past him to do so again.

When she had explained what happened he said something extremely impolite under his breath. Then the bed creaked, and to her horror his naked legs emerged from beneath the covers.

'Don't get out . . . ' Too late — he was already on his feet. Apart from a startlingly white bandage around his head, there was no indication he had been injured. Thank goodness the room was large and there were no candles lit.

'Stay where you are, sweetheart, I'm going to find my bedrobe and join you by the fire. Don't look so alarmed, I give you my word I'll not make improper advances. The last thing on my mind at the moment is making love to you.'

She wasn't sure if she was offended or relieved by his remark, and sat rigid in her chair with her eyes averted whilst he rummaged about and covered his nightgown and bare legs.

He flopped into the chair on the other side of the fire so that she had no option but to look at him. 'You have recovered remarkably quickly, Ralph. I thought you would be in bed for a day at least.'

'Half a dozen stitches and losing some blood is nothing to me — I drank a pint of watered wine to restore the balance and am now perfectly fine. I've a slight headache, but nothing worse.'

'I thought that your man would be here with you, and just came to enquire how you were doing.' She paused before deciding to continue. 'Jenkins takes too much upon himself. I shall be mistress here in a few hours, and have no intention of being ordered about by him.'

'He's devoted to me. It will take him a while to get used to the idea of me being married, but he'll adjust. If he offends you again, I'll get rid of him.'

'Oh no, I've no wish for you to dismiss him! I spoke without thinking, as I frequently do. He's a good man, and I'll learn to like him.'

He stretched out his bare toes to the fire and she couldn't help staring. She'd never seen a man's feet before, and was fascinated by the length of his toes. Her eyes drifted to his calves which were now exposed to her view.

'Verity, if you continue to look at me like that I shall forget my good intentions. It was your wish that our marriage remained in name only until we got to know each other — and I can think of no better way than by sharing the marriage bed.'

His words were like being doused in a jug of icy water. 'I beg your pardon, I must go. I find it uncomfortable being in your bedchamber when you're not dressed correctly.' She stood up, but he shook his head.

'Please stay — we have much to talk

about.' He rubbed his hand across his eyes and stared into the fire for a few seconds before continuing. 'There were rumours about this place being haunted, but I ignored them. My family abandoned the castle hundreds of years ago and I believe I now know the reason why. I've had to pay double the going wage in order to keep my staff, and to bring workmen in from fifty miles away as no local men wished to take on the repairs and renovations.'

'I don't understand why you remain here if the place is already inhabited with supernatural beings. You're a wealthy man and could live anywhere in the country.' She held up her hand as he was about to interrupt, no doubt to tell her his injuries were the reason he was a recluse. 'There are a hundred equally isolated estates available, and you could have moved to one of those. There must be another reason you've remained here.'

'You're right, of course; but it seemed appropriate to restore Castle Elrick, and for an Elrick to live here again after so long. I hasten to add that I'd no idea about the unwanted visitors until I had already committed myself.' He frowned, looking every inch the forbidding aristocrat, and for a moment she wished she'd not agreed to marry him. Then he smiled and she was glad she was here.

'At first I denied there was anything untoward going on, insisted that the strange noises were nothing more than the wind. However, after what happened this evening I'm forced to admit I was wrong.'

'I once read a book about ghosts — not a novel, but an erudite exposition about why they existed and how to remove them. If I recall correctly, ghosts are the unquiet spirits of the long departed, and they require something to be done before they can leave. Have you tried speaking to them?'

He sat forward, his expression unreadable. 'My dear girl, until today I wasn't sure they actually existed. Now I am, I think the sooner we leave here the better.

We shall be married tomorrow, and then pack up and head for my principal estate in Gloucestershire.'

'Are you suggesting that your mother and grandmother should move so that we can live at Elrick Court?'

'Good God, nothing short of an earthquake would shift either of them! However, the place is more than big enough to accommodate several families and a dozen children. Mama and Grandmamma don't occupy the main suites, so they won't have to move. They will be overjoyed to see me again, especially as I'm bringing a lovely young wife along with me. I'm the last of my line, and in every letter I receive from my parent she bemoans the fact that I have no apparent heir.'

Talking about such intimate things when they were alone together in his bedchamber made her feel lightheaded, and she thought it was time for her to retire.

'I know my duty, Ralph, and will be happy to provide you — God willing

— with a full nursery sometime in the future.' She stood up and made her way back to the exit. 'Sleep well, sir, and I shall see you in the chapel at ten o'clock.'

★ ★ ★

Ralph wanted to leap to his feet and prevent her from leaving and seduce her into his bed. It had been madness to agree to her demands: he was a red-blooded man, and it had been far too long since he'd made love to a beautiful woman.

Colonel Sanderson had described his daughter as tall, intelligent and kind; but he'd not told him she was also desirable, had eyes the colour of emeralds and glorious, nut-brown hair. He'd agreed to her stipulation that they didn't consummate the union until she felt ready, believing his future wife was a plain woman.

The moment he'd set eyes on her, his body had begun to stir in a way that he'd thought was lost to him for ever. It was going to be torture keeping her at arm's length . . . but he'd never renege on a promise. He was a gentleman, a man of honour, and would wait until she was ready to share her body with him.

He shrugged off his bedrobe and tossed it across the back of the chair and then returned to his bed. Despite his assurances to the contrary, he was feeling a trifle unsteady. He needed to get a few hours' solid sleep before telling his household that he was leaving Castle Elrick for ever.

As he was drifting into slumber, he was almost sure he heard footsteps in the passageway and voices speaking in a foreign tongue outside his door.

5

Verity slept surprisingly well and didn't wake until Sally came in with her jug of morning chocolate. 'Morning, miss, there's been over a foot of snow come down during the night. I hope the vicar can get here to marry you.'

'It's more than five miles to the nearest village so I very much doubt that he will. However, we must assume the ceremony is taking place, and I will get ready accordingly.'

Today, she didn't linger in bed to drink her chocolate, but got up immediately. There was little point in dressing until she put on her wedding finery, so she remained in her night-gown and bedrobe.

Even with the curtains pulled back, little light filtered into the room. 'I wish I could see out of the windows. I really don't like this apartment at all. Sir

76

Ralph has decided that we will remove to Elrick Court as soon as we are married, and we must start packing today.'

'From what they were saying downstairs, this weather is set in for the rest of the winter. Nobody will be going anywhere until the spring.'

The thought that she and Ralph might not be able to exchange their vows today was bad enough, but she couldn't endure a wait of several months. Although she couldn't possibly have fallen in love with him so soon, he made her pulse race, and she wished to be his true wife as soon as possible.

Then there was a loud bang on the communicating door before it swung open, revealing her future husband — in his breeches, boots and shirt. He remained in the doorway. 'Good morning, my love. I fear we'll not be able to leave Castle Elrick. However, I've sent the pony sleigh to fetch the vicar so we can be married as planned.'

'Come in, Ralph, I need to talk to you.'

He strolled in and joined her in front of the fire, but refused a bowl of chocolate when she offered it. 'I can't abide it — too thick and sickly for my taste. Now, what do you wish to speak to me about?'

'We agreed to speak honestly to each other, so I must tell you that I cannot remain in this chamber. I must be able to see out — it's like being imprisoned as it is. Is there another apartment which has more light and lower windows?'

'Is that all? Thank the good Lord — I feared you were having second thoughts about marrying me.'

'Absolutely not. I've never been more certain of anything in my life — even spectres and ghosts will not deter me.'

His smile warmed her to her very core. 'All the first-floor chambers are as gloomy; however, it wouldn't take much organisation to convert some reception rooms downstairs into an apartment.'

'Thank you, that's the best wedding gift you could give me. How long do you think it will take to rearrange things?'

'A day or two, perhaps more, depending on what you require. There is more than enough furniture, but it will have to be dismantled in order to be moved down the staircase.'

'I shall be content to remain here until it's done. At least none of your staff can desert you now we're snowed in.'

'They are your staff as well from this morning. Meet me downstairs in twenty minutes and you can select the rooms you wish to have changed. I've asked Cook to delay breakfast until after the ceremony — she's preparing something more elaborate.' He retreated into his own domain, leaving her strangely flustered.

In less than the required time, Verity was on her way, and was unsurprised to find him pacing up and down the cavernous main hall. He looked no different from normal, and she was glad she hadn't put on anything more elaborate than her moss-green ensemble.

He scarcely looked at her, merely smiled and offered his arm. She ignored this gesture and kept a safe distance between them.

'As you've no doubt noticed, only half the chambers I had modernised are in use.' He gestured towards the drawing room. 'This is the only reception room I keep heated — the breakfast parlour and the dining room also — but I don't bother with any other rooms apart from my study.'

'The rooms to the left are used for what?'

'I've no idea, I never go in them. Shall we start looking there?'

He strode across, leaving her to run behind him, and flung open the first heavy, metal-studded door, standing aside to allow her to go in first. This room had the same mullioned windows as the drawing room, and the chamber was light. Despite the icy chill, she ran forward, believing she'd found the perfect place for her new apartment.

'The view is outstanding and I should not feel imprisoned here.' She turned, and almost collided with him. For a large man with an injured leg, he moved remarkably quietly.

'This is overlarge for either a bedchamber or sitting room — it will be impossible to keep warm enough for you.' He looked around and then smiled. 'However, sweetheart, if you're determined to have this, then I can see a way we could make it work.' He pointed to the rear of the chamber. 'This could be made into your bedroom, and the other half would be your sitting room. We have a barn full of panelling that can be used for the dividing wall.'

'There are two doors at the far end. Where do they lead to? I shall need a dressing room and somewhere for my maid to work.'

He held out his hand, and this time she didn't hesitate. His fingers closed possessively around hers and he drew her close. 'We shall investigate together. I've been living here for three years but have never bothered to explore my home until now.'

The first door, somewhat smaller than the main entrance, opened into yet another flagstone passageway. He frowned. 'This must be kept locked at all times. I'm beginning to think this room won't do after all.'

Although the passage was empty, she was certain she could hear voices speaking in a language she didn't recognise. She shivered and pressed herself against him. He slammed the door and rammed the bolts across before turning back and gathering her into his arms.

'Did you hear them too?' She was safe with him; her heart stopped hammering so hard. 'I don't want to be down here on my own, Ralph.'

His arms tightened, and the buttons on his jacket pressed into her bosom. 'I've no intention of allowing you to be, my love.'

For a second, she didn't understand

his meaning, then she pushed him away. 'I hope you're not suggesting, sir, that we share this chamber? That was not the arrangement, and I expect you to keep your promise.'

Instead of being angered by her rejection, he dropped a light kiss on her brow and laughed. 'I wasn't suggesting I join you, Verity, but that your maidservant has a truckle bed in here with you.'

An uncomfortable heat spread from her toes to the crown of her head and she couldn't look at him. 'I beg your pardon, Sir Ralph. You are a gentleman, and I know that your word is your bond.'

His shout of laughter made her turn her head. 'No, sweetheart, my comment has nothing to do with my honour. I shall make love to you when the time is right, and not before.'

'Am I to have no say in the matter?' She stepped away from him and viewed him with disfavour.

His disarming grin did not help her

composure. 'Sometimes words are not necessary, sweetheart. I'm sure you understand my meaning.'

How the conversation would have developed subsequently, she had no idea, for at that moment Hodgson arrived and stared at them sourly. 'I apologise for disturbing you, Sir Ralph, but three horses and two strangers have just arrived in the stable yard, and I thought you should know at once of these unexpected visitors.'

Verity ran forward. 'I'd quite forgotten with all the excitement of the past twenty-four hours that my horses would be here this morning.' Ignoring her future husband's scowl, she rushed off to fetch her cloak so she could see how her beloved stallion had endured the journey.

Although she was gone barely ten minutes, Ralph was outside before her. He hadn't bothered to put on a coat, but had gone immediately to the stables. Fortunately, this only required a few yards' walk in the snow, as here the animals were kept in a long barn. He was talking to Fred whilst he ran his hands over Star.

The stallion, sensing his mistress's presence, barged forward, knocking both Ralph and Fred aside. He barrelled towards Verity and she threw out her arms to embrace him.

'Good day, old fellow, you obviously travelled well! I'm delighted to see you too, but please don't slobber over my cloak.'

'You forgot to mention you were bringing your own horses, Verity. Was that deliberate or an oversight?'

'Neither, Ralph, I naturally assumed my personal property could accompany me.' She was standing pressed up against the massive chest of her horse, and Star's head was resting over her shoulder. His ears were flicking back and forth, and this was a bad sign. He'd taken an instant dislike to her future husband, and that could prove disastrous.

Keeping her voice level, she tried to

explain the problem. 'Black Star is overprotective and he can be difficult if he thinks I'm in any sort of danger. Please, Ralph, move away slowly.'

His eyes darkened, but he didn't argue, and retreated until he was a safe distance away. Immediately, Star relaxed, and the danger was over.

'Why the devil is he called Black Star? The star on his face is white.'

'Yes, you're quite correct, and I'm impressed by your skills of observation. However, he *is* black and he *does* have a star, so the name is perfectly appropriate. Have you seen my two matched greys? They are Star's stable companions, and go well in harness or under saddle.'

He got the message and went into the stalls where Billy was taking care of Sultan and Sinbad. Her breath hissed through her teeth and she reached up and took hold of Star's head collar. 'Come along, I shall put you away myself. You must be on your best behaviour in your new home and not bite or kick anyone. Is that quite clear?'

Her stallion followed her, as docile as a farm horse, all signs of his previous aggression gone now that the person he saw as a threat to his owner was no longer present. By the time she'd brushed him down, and made sure he had a manger full of sweet hay and plenty of fresh water, a considerable while had passed.

Ralph was no longer in the barn. She knew he was displeased with her, and she could hardly blame him. When she stepped into the castle, Sally was waiting for her.

'Quickly, miss, the reverend gentleman is here to marry you and you can't go through as you are.'

A further fifteen minutes went by before Verity was tidy and ready to go down. She sniffed the sleeve of her gown and shook her head. 'I still smell vaguely of the stable, but I've no time to change. We must go at once, for I've kept Sir Ralph waiting long enough already.'

* * *

It was too damn cold in the small stone chapel, so they would be married in the drawing room instead. Peters, the clergyman who'd come to marry them, had viewed the special licence and declared it legitimate. All that was required now was for the bride to appear, and get this ceremony over with. Ralph had returned to the house in a foul mood, not used to being ousted by an equine, but after Jenkins had restored his appearance he had recovered his good humour.

That stallion was a magnificent beast and would breed some fine foals on his mares. It hadn't occurred to him that Verity might be an expert horsewoman, but he was delighted this was another thing they had in common. Being able to hear the voices of the resident ghosts was something else they appeared to share.

Jenkins had put things in motion for the room conversion, and thought the new partition wall would be in place by the end of the day. His man was now lurking in the corner, waiting for his role as a witness to the marriage. Later this afternoon, Verity could select the furniture she wished to have down there, tapestries could be hung on the walls, and then she could move.

He shifted uncomfortably, and hastily turned his back on the curate at the thought of sharing her bed. What he was feeling was desire . . . but that was a solid basis for a union. Maybe in time they would also come to feel affection for each other; but as long as they enjoyed making love together, the marriage would be successful.

Perhaps he would have a son or daughter next year. The thought filled him with joy. For all her faults — and they were legion — he was certain Verity would make an excellent mother and would run his household smoothly.

She was argumentative, headstrong, not at all respectful, and owned a horse that was far better than anything he'd ever possessed. He smiled to himself as he added *that* to her list of faults. However, on the plus side, she was the most desirable woman he'd ever met, and was intelligent, kind and resourceful. On balance, he rather thought he was getting more than he deserved.

If she did the same for him — how would he fare? Faults: he was autocratic, arrogant, impatient and sadly disfigured. In his favour was the fact that he remained physically strong, was wealthy, and would make a satisfactory lover. He'd certainly had no complaints from the women he'd bedded in the past.

At last he could hear her approaching. He turned to Peters, and the man straightened and opened his prayer at the appropriate page. Verity burst in.

'I apologise for my tardiness, Sir Ralph, I spent too long in the stables.'

'Indeed you did, my dear, and in future would do better to leave such tasks to the men I employ to do them.' He had not meant to sound so abrupt and her smile faded. He must do better than this if he was to woo her into his bed.

He held out his hand, but for the second time this morning she ignored it and stood beside him, eyes to the front, her displeasure obvious. They spoke their vows, he pushed a plain gold band onto her wedding finger, and the deed was done.

It was as if everyone held their breath waiting to see if he would kiss the bride. Devil take it! Their arrangement was private and he had no intention of allowing anyone else to learn that the marriage was not to be consummated until his bride agreed.

He was still holding her hand, and he raised it to his lips and kissed the ring. 'It might seem unlikely, sweetheart, but I will make you an excellent husband, and promise that you'll never regret your decision to marry me.'

This comment had the desired effect, and for the first time since the cere-mony had begun she looked directly at him. Her eyes glittered with unshed tears and he considered how she must be feeling. All young ladies dreamt of marrying, but this dream would not have envisaged a ceremony such as this without family or friends in attendance, and with no wedding breakfast or celebration to mark the occasion.

She blinked and somehow managed a weak smile. 'I promise I'll be a good wife to you, and my tears are for my father who cannot be here to witness this event. It was his wish that we married, and he would not have arranged it if he didn't think we would suit.'

He slipped his free arm around her waist and drew her closer. Her eyes widened when she realised his intention but she didn't pull away. She tilted her head and he kissed her. For a glorious few moments he forgot they were strangers, that they were to remain apart, and revelled in the sensation. Her mouth softened beneath his and the blood surged through his veins.

Then he regained control and held

her at arm's length. 'An interesting perfume, my love, not something one would expect from one's bride.' He shook his head and pulled a comical face.

She giggled and snatched her hands back. 'Oh dear! I had no time to change and feared I would smell of the stables. I hope you don't wish me to rectify the matter immediately, as I'm sharp-set and wish to break my fast.'

He offered his arm and this time she took it immediately. 'Then we shall eat, sweetheart. I must say, I prefer a young lady with a healthy appetite.'

She peeked at him through her eyelashes. 'Another compliment? I'm quite overwhelmed by your charm, Sir Ralph; I cannot remember any gentleman telling me before that I smell unpleasant and am also greedy.'

'Saucy minx. I can see that I'm going to have my work cut out bringing you to heel.'

This time she laughed out loud and he didn't, at first, see why she had found his remark so funny. Then she enlightened him.

'I'm not a canine to be trained, sir, and if you thought otherwise then I fear you've married the wrong woman.'

'No, Lady Elrick, I've made the perfect choice.'

6

Despite the irregularity of the ceremony, and the strange occurrences of the previous day, the castle almost had a festive mood. The various members of staff they passed bowed, curtsied and smiled, and by the time they reached the breakfast parlour Verity was feeling almost jolly.

'Good gracious me! Look at the spread set out for us this morning — at least we can be sure your staff will also benefit from our nuptials.'

They piled their plates and carried them to the table, which had been laid up with the best silver cutlery and adorned with a sparkling white cloth. There was coffee and chocolate to drink, as well as small beer, and a strange herbal version of lemonade.

Once she was replete, she put down her knife and fork ready to discuss how they should proceed. 'Ralph, if we're obliged to stay here until the spring, what are we going to do about the unwanted visitors? Are your staff aware that we are both hearing and seeing supernatural occurrences?'

He swallowed his mouthful and wiped his lips on his napkin. 'It's not something I care to discuss with them. These past three years, I've been pretending there's nothing untoward taking place here. Until yesterday, the ghosts were never heard or seen, apart from the odd noise or two on the battlements. I think we must resign ourselves to celebrating Christmas and New Year at Castle Elrick. I've instructed Saxton to decorate the place as best she can, and we have a yule log ready to go in the fireplace in the hall.'

She was impressed. 'I saw no woods in the vicinity so where were these items found?'

'You've not had time to ride around my demesne, so didn't see that I have an acre or so of hardy trees growing inland no more than a mile from here. Everything that's needed was collected several days ago whilst the weather was still clement.'

'I'd hardly call the lack of snow a reason for calling it clement, Ralph. However, I'll not cavil; I must become used to Northumbrian ways for the present.' She poured herself a second cup of coffee before mentioning something that had been on her mind since her encounter with the ghosts last evening.

'I heard them talking — they were not speaking in English. The reason I fell had nothing to do with them: I missed my step when the lights went out.'

'I thought the same. How curious! As far as I know, only Elricks have ever lived here, and the language the spectres spoke was definitely foreign — but not French, Spanish or Italian, as I can speak a smattering of all those.'

'Another thing — I had the distinct impression the door and staircase have something to do with them. Shall we go and investigate?'

He pointed to the swirling whiteness outside the windows. 'There's nothing else we can do until the snow stops. I fear the unfortunate clergyman will be obliged to stay with us, but at least that means he can lead us in prayer on Christmas Day.'

'The poor man must be upset at being snowed in. I hope the house-keeper has found him a comfortable room. He must dine with us tonight, of course, and maybe his presence will deter the ghosts from another appear-ance.'

Ralph stared at her as if she were a simpleton. 'Dine with us? Good God — I should think not. I share my table with no one apart from family and friends, and he is quite definitely neither.'

'I believe this is to be our first argument as man and wife. I'm afraid I must insist that he joins us this evening. He is a guest under our roof and will be treated with respect. You must put your personal feelings to one side and not be so curmudgeonly. In two days' time we will be celebrating the Lord's birthday: it's hardly the season for being grudging and inhospitable.' For a horrible moment she thought she'd overstepped the mark, but then he smiled and nodded his acceptance.

'You're right, sweetheart, it's hardly the wretched man's fault he's stuck here. Anyway, he'll fare a lot better at Castle Elrick than he would in his own modest lodgings.' He stood up and was behind her chair before she could move. 'Allow me, my dear, to assist you to your feet.'

'Don't be ridiculous, Ralph, I'm perfectly capable of getting up and down without your help. By the way, that reminds me — what happened to your bandage and your stitches? Turn your head and let me see.'

Obediently, he did as she asked, and she could just discern the sutures beneath his thick, black hair. 'I'd almost forgotten about my injury — apart from a slight headache, I've no ill effects at all. Now, shall we go and investigate this mysterious moving staircase, or do you have something else you would rather do?'

'Staircase first, and then I wish to help with the decorations. I've never been in a house where Christmas is celebrated in the old-fashioned way, and I'm really looking forward to seeing this place come alive when it's decked with festive greenery. I'm hoping that you'll join me — after all, it's a bride's prerogative to have her own way on her wedding day.'

This time she slipped her arm through his without being asked, and they made their way to the rear of the building. 'It's much quieter here, and not because it's unoccupied — there's an absence of any sort of noise, don't you think?'

He tilted his head and listened carefully, then nodded. 'You're quite correct, sweetheart; it's unnaturally quiet. However, the silence is peaceful and not particularly threatening.'

He led her into the passageway where he'd had his accident the night before, and the doorway leading to the stairs was immediately visible. 'It looks perfectly normal, not moving about or behaving in a mysterious way,' Verity reflected. 'I've no wish to open the door, I shall leave that to you.'

She peered into the gloom of the stairwell when he opened it, and all appeared as it should. 'Shall we go up them?'

'Not without a lamp — but they certainly look like an ordinary set of stairs.'

'We can see almost to the top with the door open. I'll hold it and you can explore.'

He took her suggestion seriously. 'You're right, but you must remain out here, whatever happens.' He grinned and looked years younger. It was strange, but she no longer noticed the scar on his face or the fact that he limped.

'Be careful, Ralph, I've no wish to be a widow so soon in our relationship.' Her comment was intended to lighten the mood, but it did something else entirely. He turned, and before she could protest she was in his arms.

'So we have a relationship? I'm delighted to hear it, my love, and intend to pursue the idea in more detail at a more convenient time.' Then he kissed her hard and released her, laughing at her bemused expression.

There was no time to respond as he vanished up the stairs, leaving her to hang on to the door as much for support as to keep it open.

Then, to her horror, the door moved of its own volition, and she was pushed forward at such speed she couldn't prevent herself from tumbling headlong through the opening. The door slammed shut behind her, leaving her in darkness.

For a moment she couldn't breathe — too petrified to do more than huddle on her knees. Then Ralph's voice came from just above her. 'Buggeration! I can't see a damn thing here — is anybody there?'

Hearing him using such appalling language roused her from her terror. 'Yes, I'm here, and there's no need to swear.' She tried to move backwards, but appeared to be held by some invisible force.

'Stay where you are, sweetheart, I'm coming down. What happened? Why did the door close so suddenly?'

He was beside her before he'd finished his sentence, and his arms reached out and pulled her onto his lap. 'Something or someone pushed me forwards, and the door closed behind me. I couldn't move until you picked me up. It's so dark that I've no idea in which direction I'm facing.' She settled more comfortably, enjoying the intimacy of the darkness and the warmth of his solid embrace. 'It's strange . . . although we appear to be trapped here in the dark, I don't feel at all scared — in fact, quite the reverse.'

'You're right — wherever we are, I'm certain we're in no danger.' He pulled her closer and whispered, 'I'm going to try and communicate with whatever is holding us here.'

Verity held her breath and waited to see what he intended to say to these invisible beings who had the power to imprison them.

'I am Ralph Elrick, owner of this castle, a descendant of the original family who built it centuries ago. Who are you and what do you want from us?'

The hair on the back of her neck stood to attention, and there was that familiar murmur of voices in the language she didn't recognise. Then Ralph's arms tightened. He must have seen something. She turned her head: there, shimmering in the darkness, were two shapes.

Her bladder almost emptied, and she closed her eyes and buried her face in Ralph's shoulder. However benign they might be, she'd no wish to converse with ghosts!

He appeared unbothered by the circumstances. 'Good day to you. I fear you speak in a tongue I don't understand. We will help you if we can, but have no idea what it is you want.'

Something brushed past her face, and she couldn't hold back her scream. When she opened her eyes, she was sitting on the flagstones in the passageway, and the door was no longer there.

* * *

Ralph clutched at Verity, but she'd gone. He was on his feet, and about to dive head-first towards where the door should be, when something touched his shoulder and his fear and anger dissipated. For some reason he was certain she was unharmed.

And he was alone — well, without human contact, but there were definitely other beings hovering about. He'd faced many dangerous situations in the past without flinching, but squaring up to ghosts was something quite different.

'What do you want from me? I cannot understand the language you're speaking.'

A ghostly finger brushed his face, and although he didn't recognise the words he found he could understand the gist of what was being said. He wasn't sure if actual words were being spoken or the thoughts were being put into his head.

'You want me to dig up your bones and put them in a boat, set fire to it and send them out to sea? You were Viking raiders who died here at the hands of my ancestors, but never received your ritual burial, and cannot leave for Valhalla until this has been done?'

The strange voices buzzed in his head and he knew he'd understood correctly. The mortal remains of these ghosts had been tossed into a makeshift grave outside the castle walls.

'I give you my word that as soon as I can, I'll do as you ask. Will you then vacate this property and leave us in peace?'

He was enveloped by a swirl of ghostly figures and knew he'd satisfied their demands. He was about to ask why they had taken so long to speak to him when he had been in residence for more than three years, when the floor beneath him shifted and he found himself outside in the passageway.

Before he could adjust to his rapid change of environment, Verity landed in his lap and flung her arms around his neck in a most unexpected and exceedingly pleasurable way.

'I thought you gone for ever, swallowed up by the ghosts! The door has disappeared again. Did they tell you what they wanted?'

Having her warm weight pressing against his nether regions was about to cause them both embarrassment. He tipped her off and pushed himself upright before grabbing her hand and doing the same for her. He explained what the ghosts wanted and she nodded.

'Considering the Vikings were a murderous lot on the whole, we're very lucky to have such well-behaved ghosts living here. This is going to be a most enjoyable Christmas after all, and we can forget about what's happened and concentrate on preparing the castle.'

He was still holding her hand, loving the softness of her skin against his rough palm. 'I don't believe there's another young lady in the country who would dismiss a castle full of dead Vikings with such aplomb. They might appear benign, but I've a feeling they are mischievous, and we might yet have more interference to come.'

'I think you should tell the staff who they are . . . '

'Good God! Have you run mad? If we confirmed their fears they would all leave, despite the snow. There's no such thing as a good ghost as far as the folk around here are concerned. We shall keep this matter to ourselves until we're in a position to do something about it — in other words, not for several weeks.'

'Very well, I must bow to your

superior knowledge of your servants. Now, I wish to see how the conversion is progressing, and also to select the furniture I wish to have in my new apartment.'

'I suppose I'd better find the preacher and make sure he's comfortable. Perhaps he plays billiards or *vingt-et-un* and will give me a game or two.'

'A clergyman gambling? I hardly think so. He's probably hiding in the freezing library reading a suitably serious religious tract.'

They had now reached the main hall, and the sound of hammering ruled out the possibility of further conversation. She released his hand, and with a friendly wave picked up her skirts and ran across to vanish into the room that was to be hers.

The housekeeper glided up beside him and curtsied. 'Excuse me, Sir Ralph, we have prepared the garlands and wreaths and would like to start putting them in place. Would you have any objection if that is done now?'

'Go ahead, Saxton, you have my permission to do whatever is necessary to make this draughty old place look more festive.' She curtsied again and was about to leave when he called her back. 'Have you any idea where the clergyman is hiding?'

'He's gone, Sir Ralph. He refused to remain here after the ceremony, and said he would walk to the village as no one was prepared to take him.'

Ralph muttered imprecations under his breath and headed immediately for the stables. By the time he reached them, he was covered in snow, and hoped no one had been foolish enough to venture out in this blizzard. He could only think of one reason why the wretched man had been so determined to leave Castle Elrick — he must have had an encounter with a ghost. Why else would he risk his life or that of anyone else in order to return to his dismal cottage in such a hurry?

Fortunately, the stables were under cover, as they were a series of loose boxes constructed in an open barn. The carriage house was adjacent and he was relieved to see the sleigh was still in place. Thank the Lord no one had gone out in this appalling weather — if they had, they were unlikely to survive.

Jim Roberts met him, and one look at his grim expression sent shivers down Ralph's spine. 'Mr Peters has disappeared, sir, we can't find him anywhere. I told him we couldn't take him back today, that he would perish if he tried to walk, and I thought he'd accepted what I said. However, I fear he set off on his own.'

'Have you searched the castle and the grounds?'

'We've done what we can, sir, but any footprints he might have left would have been covered immediately by the falling snow. I was about to come and find you and ask what we should do next.'

'We can't leave him to die out there. Give me a quarter of an hour to get myself ready, and then we must take a search party — and pray we find him and don't die in the process. Saddle up the four draft horses, and put blankets over their rumps and forequarters to protect them from the worst of the elements. Do the same for yourself and two others.'

This was not how he had expected to spend his wedding day. First he had an encounter with a horde of Viking ghosts, and then the man who'd married him to Verity had decided to commit suicide rather than remain under the same roof as these dead warriors.

7

Verity was impressed with the industry of the carpenters, and was assured by the foreman that the work would be done by the next day. Already the few pieces of furniture that had been left in this empty chamber had been removed. There were also smaller partition walls being placed in the sleeping end of the apartment for a dressing room and workroom for Sally.

Her next task would be to find the items she wished to have down here, and she thought she would ask the housekeeper for advice. She found Saxton in her office, working at a large ledger.

'You should have rung for me, my lady, I don't expect you to come and find me.'

'I shall do so in future, but I'm here now.' She explained the reason for her visit and Saxton was delighted to leave her work in order to accompany Verity upstairs.

'Is Mr Peters comfortably settled? Sir Ralph and I wish him to enjoy his enforced stay and hope he will join us for dinner tonight.'

'He isn't staying, my lady, he was adamant he was returning to the village. He left the castle a while ago.'

'Sir Ralph said anyone going out in this blizzard would perish. I must find my husband and tell him. God willing, we will find Mr Peters before he sets off on his own.'

She rushed into her apartment and shouted for her maid to bring her cloak and bonnet immediately. Within minutes she was suitably clothed and on her way to the rear of the building, relieved she would not have to be exposed to the elements for more than a few yards.

Ralph was talking earnestly to three well-muffled men — he was obviously going in search of the missing man. He saw her at once and strode towards her.

'You shouldn't be out here, sweetheart, the weather is vile. I suppose you've come to tell me the wretched curate has vanished.'

'I have. I don't want you to go out yourself, it's far too dangerous. Mr Peters decided to leave; he must have known the risks, and should be left to his own devices. Surely it's not right for others to lose their lives because of his foolishness?'

'I have no choice: as long as there's a faint chance we can find him and bring him back alive, we must make the effort. Don't forget I've lived here for three winters, and have had to go out in worse than this on occasion, and survived the experience.'

There was nothing she could say to dissuade him. This might be the last time she saw him and she wished him to know he was already an important part of her life. She stepped closer and stood on tiptoes so she could kiss his lips. They were cold beneath hers. 'Take care, Ralph, I want you back safely.'

'I have something to live for now: I can assure you I've no intention of kicking the bucket today.' He swung athletically into the saddle, tied his muffler around his face and over his head, then rammed his beaver on top. With his many-caped driving coat spread out behind him to keep his horse warm, and his face obscured, he was no longer recognisable.

The small cavalcade moved forward, but as they reached the exit a snow-encrusted figure tottered around the corner and collapsed in front of them. The missing curate had miraculously returned. Verity sent a quick prayer of thanks to the Almighty and ran forward to offer what assistance she could.

The poor man was so cold his lips were blue and there were icicles hanging from his eyebrows. He was incapable of speech.

'Mr Peters, let me help you inside. You should never have ventured out in a blizzard, and are fortunate to have been able to return safely.' She was about to reach down and help him to his feet when Ralph gripped her around the waist and lifted her out of the way. He then picked up the unfortunate clergyman and tossed him over his shoulder like a sack of potatoes.

The curate was too cold and demoralised to protest at this cavalier treatment. Verity followed them inside, but by the time she had removed her snow-covered cloak and bonnet and handed them to a waiting chamber-maid, Ralph had disappeared with his burden.

It was probably best to leave Mr Peters in the hands of her husband as he would not enjoy being attended to by a lady. She hoped the silly man wouldn't attempt to escape again, and wondered if his mind would be eased if they explained the ghosts would do him no harm.

When she thought about it logically she realised that the existence of beings from the afterlife was no more remarkable than the birth of Christ. These ghosts were pagans, so didn't believe in the Holy Trinity — however, they would appreciate having evergreens around the place and a yule log burning on tomorrow's winter solstice.

The housekeeper — having settled Mr Peters and ensured he had dry clothes, hot food and a warm chamber — joined Verity to continue the search for items to go in the new apartment.

'I think I have enough furniture, thank you, Saxton. I'm delighted with the carpets and tapestries you've shown me, and happy for you to arrange for my books and personal effects to be moved tomorrow. With all the fires lit, the rooms will be delightfully warm when I get there.'

The housekeeper curtsied. 'Are you happy with the arrangement of the evergreens, my lady? Perhaps you would like to oversee the decorations yourself, if you can spare the time?'

'I should love to. Do we have

sufficient candles to put in the garlands? I've no wish for us to run short this winter.'

'We have a surfeit of everything, my lady, Sir Ralph insisted that we fill up the storerooms, larders and coal hole with enough to last us for a siege. He has been sending for luxury items since last spring.'

The housekeeper hurried off, leaving Verity to make her own way. So Ralph had been planning for her arrival for months: she wasn't sure if she was perturbed or pleased by this information. She was still at a loss to comprehend why such an attractive gentleman could believe he was so disfigured he could no longer appear in society. The only explanation she could think of was that he had had such a high opinion of his appearance before his injuries that he couldn't accept his perfection had been marred.

Her heart skipped a beat, and she sent her love and thanks to her dear departed father for sending her to

Northumbria. She wasn't a foolish girl; after all, she was already well past the age that most young ladies were married, and knew she couldn't possibly have fallen in love with her husband so quickly. Although she knew little of the secrets of the marriage bed, she had seen animals mating and understood the rudiments of the process.

But she hadn't realised that just the thought of sharing her body with him would make her tingle with anticipation. This was not love, but lust, and a proper young lady would not give in to such base feelings. She must make every effort to remain aloof from him, to avoid any physical contact. Mr Peters would be joining them for dinner, which meant that she would be safe from temptation this evening.

There was no luncheon served in the small dining room that day, as Verity was far too busy directing and supervising the arrangement of the beautiful garlands, candles, wreaths and ribbons. Ralph wandered in and out occasionally to compliment the decorations, and Mr Peters had a tray sent to his chamber.

Once the workmen had finished for the day, the curtains were drawn and the castle was quiet. The huge log burning in the hall made the vast space a little warmer, but still not somewhere one would wish to linger. Every available surface was festooned with greenery into which had been pushed magnificent beeswax candles and dozens of red, green and gold ribbons tied in rosettes and bows. The candles would be lit on Christmas Eve and Verity couldn't wait to see them flickering around the place.

There was only an hour before dinner would be served, so she should return to her rooms and change or she would be tardy. Instead, she made her way to the study in the hope that her errant husband was hiding there. She knocked on the door and was pleased to be asked to enter.

'Come in, sweetheart, I was just thinking about you.' He stood up and came to greet her with his hand outstretched.

Her intention had been to avoid touching him, but it would be churlish to refuse this gesture of friendship.

His fingers closed around hers and a pulse of heat ran up her arm. 'I was thinking I might put on an evening gown tonight; after all, it is our wedding day.'

'Then I shall change as well. Hodgson has told me our guest is indisposed with a head cold so we will have dinner alone.'

She attempted to remove her hand, but his fingers tightened, making this impossible. 'I've changed my mind; I'll keep my finery until our guest is well enough to join us.' She schooled her features into indifference. 'After all, I've no need to impress you. We are merely strangers who have entered into a mutually agreeable business transaction, and are indifferent to each other.'

'Are we indeed? Perhaps that was the case before we met, but I can assure you the last thing I feel for you is indifference. I give you fair warning, my love, that I wish to make this a true marriage, and intend to do everything in my power to persuade you to change your mind.' His thumb was tracing circles on her palm and his eyes were soft and dark — he was irresistible.

Then a gust of wind came down the chimney, covering them in acrid smoke, and he was forced to let her go. She fled before she could say — or do — something she would later regret.

She paused on the stairs to gaze around the ancient hall with its gleaming armour and weapons of war. A week ago, she had not even known of the existence of this place and its owner — and yet she was now married to him, and already tempted to make the union genuine.

Sally greeted her with enthusiasm. 'My lady, I can scarcely believe how this place has changed since we arrived. You know, even the servants' hall has been decorated, and everyone is ever so jolly. I've never eaten so well in my life as I have here.'

'I believe I could come to like it here very well, despite the obvious drawbacks. It's amazing what a cartload of evergreens and a box of ribbons can do to cheer a place up. I'm not sure if I wish to go down for dinner — I'm feeling a little overwhelmed by it all.'

'I'm not surprised, my lady, you've been busy all day and didn't even stop to eat at midday. I'll send a girl down for a supper tray. You curl up on the daybed with your book; there's a lovely fire in your sitting room. I'll make sure Mr Hodgson tells the master you won't be coming down tonight.'

Just in case Ralph decided to come and fetch her, Verity changed into her nightwear and put on a negligée in the certainty that he could hardly insist she joined him downstairs. Sally returned saying she'd delivered the message, and that there would be no formal dinner tonight as everyone was dining from a tray.

'That's good news indeed. I should hate Sir Ralph to have been in his evening finery on his own. I'll make an effort tomorrow. I've brought three evening gowns with me, and all have matching shawls, so I won't freeze.'

* * *

Jenkins brought Ralph the message that Verity was dining in her room just before he began to change. 'Tell Hodgson I'll not be coming down again, so he can lock up and the staff can have a relatively free evening.'

'I'll do that, sir, but there's something I need to know. Did Mr Peters explain how he found his way back?'

'I've yet to ask him — he was in no fit state to be questioned when I carried him to his chamber. Does it matter?'

His valet's expression was dour. 'There's talk downstairs of strange men being seen out in the snow: men with axes, metal helmets, and long flaxen hair. I reckon you'll lose most of the staff when they can leave here safely. Them ghosts might be friendly, but

125

ordinary folks are still afeard of such beings.'

'I hardly think it matters now, as I intend to move back to Gloucestershire in the spring, and would have to dismiss the locals anyway. As long as a handful remain, we'll manage perfectly well.'

'The men what came with us will stay — that's seven of us — but I don't reckon many of the indoor staff will.'

'I don't suppose that telling them we have a jolly lot of Vikings, nothing evil or unpleasant about them, would make any difference?'

'Doubt it — don't think it matters what sort of ghosts they are. I'm not too bothered meself — I've seen and heard a few strange things in my life, and I'm none the worse for it.'

Ralph was damned if he was going to eat on his own when he had a perfectly good wife to converse with. 'Tell the kitchen to send my supper to Lady Elrick's apartment. I shan't need you again tonight, Jenkins; you can serve me best downstairs reassuring those that want to turn tail and run once the weather improves.'

He checked his neckcloth was neatly tied, his waistcoat buttoned, and he was ready to depart. He smiled to himself as he knocked on the communicating door. He waited impatiently but no one came to answer it. He lifted the latch but the door didn't budge; Verity had pushed the bolt across. Undeterred, he walked through into his sitting room, out of the door, and along the corridor to her sitting room.

He was about to knock, then hesitated. Surely as master of the house he could enter any room without permission? He wouldn't dream of going into her bedchamber uninvited, but thought it perfectly reasonable to do so anywhere else.

He compromised, and knocked and opened simultaneously. Verity was curled up on the *chaise longue*, staring pensively into the fire, the book on her lap forgotten. She jerked upright at the sudden sound, sending the book flying. He watched in dismay as it arced through the air and landed square in the grate.

Without conscious thought, he was across the room and reaching into the fire to rescue it. Although smouldering a little around the edges, it was still perfectly readable.

She had tumbled from the daybed and was beside him in seconds. She grabbed the slightly singed book and tossed it aside, then took his hands in hers and began to examine them. 'Ralph, you shouldn't have done that! You could have been severely burned — I'd rather lose a dozen novels than have you hurt.'

His heart was pounding, and it wasn't from his close encounter with the flames. The more he saw her, the more he wanted to make love to her. 'The accident was my fault so I had to do what I could to remedy the situation.' He gently pulled his hands away and showed first the palms and then the backs. 'See, sweetheart, perfectly fine.

I've come to eat with you. Shall we move that table in front of the fire, and then I'll put two chairs ready for when the trays arrive.'

She didn't look overjoyed at his announcement. 'I don't recall inviting you here, sir, and I'm not sure it's a good idea for us to be closeted together when I am improperly dressed.'

He ignored her comment and proceeded to do as he suggested. By the time he'd arrange the furniture to his satisfaction, the food had arrived. He'd asked for champagne as well as orgeat, and this was placed with due ceremony on a side table. He checked the temperature of the bottle and was satisfied it was cold enough.

Two parlourmaids deftly spread the table with a sparkling white cloth. One put out cutlery, crystalware and china, whilst another laid a tempting array of dishes on the sideboard. This girl curtsied nervously.

'Do you wish us to stay and serve you, Sir Ralph?'

'No, run along. We will not require you again tonight — you can collect the trays first thing tomorrow morning.'

He half-expected Verity to have disappeared whilst she had the chance, but the appetising aromas wafting across the room must have overcome her reluctance to eat in private with him. He didn't blame her one jot; the way he felt about his new wife, it would take only the smallest encouragement for him to carry her to bed.

8

Verity had never been so flustered in her life before — what was it about this man that so unsettled her? Was it possible that she was beginning to have feelings for him? It hardly seemed credible that after spending just two days in his company, not only was he her husband, but he was also becoming her friend . . . and, if she wasn't very careful, he would soon be her lover too.

She couldn't take her eyes from him as he rearranged the furniture to his satisfaction, then as the maids did their work and he dismissed them. If he hadn't been so grievously wounded, she would never have met him; so she was glad that he had received those injuries and that her father had been able to save his life.

These reprehensible thoughts had slipped unwanted into her mind, and she was deeply ashamed of them. She had never thought of herself as a selfish person, but this proved that she was. She blinked back tears and wondered if she could surreptitiously wipe her eyes on her sleeve.

He swung round and was at her side in an instant. He took her hands in his and gently squeezed them. 'What's wrong, my love? I should never have foisted myself on you like this. I'll get myself something to eat and take it next door and leave you alone.'

She spoke what was in her heart. 'No, please stay. I'm not upset about that, but about the dreadful things I was thinking.'

'Move up a little and let me sit down beside you. Are you concerned about ghosts?'

She shifted along the daybed making room for him and wished she'd held her peace. 'I'm not worried about them, not anymore. Like you I believe they have no evil intentions, but are merely trapped in our dimension until you've performed the burial rites they require.'

'Then what is it? I know we've only known each other a short while, but you can trust me. I want us to be friends, to be honest with each other, and keeping secrets isn't a good start to our married life.'

There was no option, she must explain; but she couldn't look him in the eye as she told him. 'I was thinking that I was glad you had been injured because otherwise we would never have met.' There — she'd said it, and now he would hold her in disgust. She waited for him to withdraw, to give her the scathing set-down she so richly deserved.

To her astonishment and delight, he reached over and picked her up, then placed her on his lap. However, instead of answering her with words, he cupped the back of her head and tilted her face towards him so he could kiss her.

This wasn't like his previous kisses: his lips were hard, demanding, the tip of his tongue pressing against her lips. Her mouth opened of its own volition, then he was plundering the inner moistness, and something strong and powerful surged around her body.

She arched her back, pressing against him, and her hands slid out to become entangled in the soft hair at the nape of his neck. Every inch of her was aflame and she didn't want him to stop. Then, to her dismay, he drew back and she was bereft.

His eyes were dark, his hair ruffled, and a hectic flush ran across his cheekbones. He was breathtakingly beautiful, and she knew in that instant she was where she was meant to be. This was the man she'd been waiting for — the man who would make her a woman.

'I don't want to rush things, my darling, I promised to wait until we knew each other better. I've no wish for you to have regrets.'

She was still dizzy with excitement and could scarcely catch her breath enough to answer. 'I know what I said in my letter, but I've changed my mind.

There's a connection between us — it might only be passion, but as we are husband and wife I can see no reason to deny ourselves.'

His smile curled her toes. 'In which case, I suggest we dine and drink a toast to the start of our life together.'

Verity scarcely noticed what she ate, and the champagne was a delicious accompaniment to the meal. She enjoyed it so much that she refilled her glass more than once when she was unobserved. There was something pertinent she wished to say, but for the life of it she couldn't remember. Then she recalled what it was. 'Tomorrow is Christmas Eve, we must light all the candles to celebrate our marriage and the birth of our Lord.' For some reason, Ralph's face was moving from place to place in a most disconcerting way. She screwed up her eyes in the hope that this would make things clearer. It didn't, and her stomach lurched.

He reached out and removed the half-full glass of champagne from her hand. 'I think you've had far too much of this, sweetheart. I should never have let you help yourself.'

She clapped her hands to her mouth. 'I never drink alcohol, it doesn't agree with me.'

His expression changed from amused to alarmed. 'Devil take it! Hang on a minute, I'll find a suitable receptacle.'

He produced a basin in the nick of time. After an extremely unpleasant five minutes she was done. Her head was spinning like a top and she still felt decidedly peculiar.

'Come along, I think it's time you went to bed. I warn you that you'll have a nasty headache in the morning.' He scooped her up, and she felt too unwell to do more than flop against his shoulder. He removed her negligée with expert hands, and then put her into bed as if she were a small child again.

'I'm sorry . . . '

'Don't apologise, my love; we have the rest of our lives together, so there's no need to rush into anything.'

She watched with blurry eyes as he placed an empty bowl within hand's reach, and wished with all her heart that this evening had ended differently. As she drifted into sleep, she heard him unbolt the communicating door, and that was the last thing she knew until the morning.

★ ★ ★

Ralph left the door ajar as he went into his own bedchamber — he wanted to be able to hear if Verity was ill again. He smiled ruefully. This was hardly the romantic ending she'd anticipated for her wedding night! He hoped she wouldn't be too embarrassed when she woke in the morning, but he hadn't been at all disgusted by her casting up her accounts. He'd seen and dealt with far worse during his many years as a soldier.

He tossed his jacket, waistcoat and neckcloth in a heap on the floor, his mind preoccupied with more important matters than offending his valet. When Verity had said she was glad she'd met him, he'd never felt such joy. There'd been a string of ladybirds over the years, of course — what gentleman didn't keep a mistress or two? However, previously he'd thought love between adults was but flummery, and best kept between the covers of the romantic novels young ladies were disposed to read.

This lump in his chest, the way his pulse raced every time he saw her, and that he would willingly die for her — and just as willingly kill any man who dared to harm a hair on her head — could only be caused by one thing. He had been afflicted by the great malady — romantic love, from which he was certain there would be no cure.

How this could have happened in so short a space of time, he was at a loss to understand; but happened it had, and his life was changed forever. He didn't give a damn about his appearance anymore and was certain that even when Verity saw the hideous scar that ran across his stomach, she wouldn't be repulsed.

Ghosts, benevolent or evil, were of no matter. He was invincible, could conquer any obstacle!

It was far too early to retire, and he'd sent his staff to bed so could hardly disturb them again. There was a lamp in his dressing room that Jenkins used when traversing the dark servants' staircase: if he used that, he could go downstairs to the study and find something to do there.

The fact that there would be a decanter of brandy on the sideboard was another incentive to venture out into the freezing passageways in his breeches and bedrobe. Thank God he'd had the foresight to leave his boots on.

The castle was eerily silent considering the time was only ten o'clock — he couldn't remember ever wandering around the place when the wall sconces were out and there wasn't a single member of staff on duty. He emerged from the stone staircase into the grand hall, and held his oil lamp aloft to admire the festive decorations.

The enormous log burning in the grate made this space a little lighter than everywhere else, and certainly a lot warmer. He walked into the centre, and shards of light reflected on the suits of armour, making them seem almost alive.

The passageway leading to the study was dark and unpleasantly cold. He increased his pace — no point in lingering down here when he had a comfortable sitting room upstairs. He lifted the latch on the heavy door and pushed, but it didn't budge. Puzzled, he put down the lamp so he could put his shoulder to it.

On the second attempt it flew open and he fell head-first into the room. It was like pitching into Stygian darkness . . . and he wasn't alone. He was on his feet in seconds, tense, not sure what had alerted him. Then something brushed against his face and the hair on his forearms stood to attention.

Only then did he realise the door had closed behind him. He was surrounded by the Elrick Vikings, and he'd no notion how to deal with spectres. He steadied his breathing and was about to speak when he was spoken to. Not audibly, but the words were clear in his mind.

'*Welcome — we wish you no harm. We hope that you enjoy your yuletide festivities. You have given your vow to send us to join our forefathers, and we wish to know when this will take place.*'

For a moment, Ralph couldn't think of a response. Last time he'd heard these ghosts, they had been incomprehensible; and yet here they were, communicating with him in plain English, and didn't sound at all like the murderous invaders he'd read about in books.

'*We have been able to communicate in your tongue for centuries, but chose not to until now. Not all of us were rapists and murderers — we were* raiders, but killed only those who fought against us. We did not die with our swords in our hands, so could not travel to Valhalla and join our ancestors. You must rectify this.'

'Why haven't you asked for assistance before this? I've been here for several years and have been well aware I wasn't alone in the castle.'

'You have only become receptive since your soulmate arrived two days ago. We have tried over the centuries to communicate with the occupants of the castle, but only succeeded in driving them from here.'

'I can do nothing until the snow clears, but you will receive your burial rites as soon as it does. Could I ask you to remain invisible to all but myself and my wife? My staff are about to desert me en masse, as even benevolent ghosts are unacceptable to them. If this happens, then I'll not be able to remain here myself.'

The room flickered strangely, and suddenly he was surrounded by half a dozen ghostly figures. They seemed less friendly and more menacing.

'*We have waited long enough, and are not prepared to wait much longer. When your yuletide festivities are over we expect you to do as we ask.*'

There was no necessity for him to answer, they could read his thoughts. He snatched up the decanter of brandy and headed for the door, which opened of its own volition and closed behind him. He looked at the brandy and realised he'd forgotten to pick up a glass. He frowned, then decided he would rather drink from the decanter than go back into the study.

The oil lamp he'd placed on the floor was still burning brightly, a welcome oasis of light in the dark. As he stooped to pick it up, he felt a prickle of awareness slither up his spine. Then, to his astonishment, there was a glass beside the lamp. He grabbed it, made his way briskly to the central hall, and was back in his apartment in double-quick time.

With shaking hands he poured himself a generous measure of brandy and gulped it down. Ghosts were bad enough, but ghosts that could move physical objects at random were quite terrifying. He flopped into the nearest chair, still clutching the decanter and glass. Finally he understood just how dangerous the situation was. These unwelcome visitors could use any of the weapons that decorated the castle walls to commit murder whenever they wished.

He poured himself a second drink and emptied the glass. He would rather deal with one hundred Frenchies than a handful of ghosts. The leader of this ethereal band had only fetched the glass to demonstrate the power they had. This was a warning that they could wreak havoc, and would only hold back until after Christmas.

With two foot of snow outside, he couldn't make a run for it. He would talk to Jenkins tomorrow and hope they could come up with a plan of action that would keep everyone safe until the bones could be dug up and sent out to sea.

When the decanter was empty he fell into a deep, alcoholic sleep, still with his boots on.

* * *

Verity slept fitfully and woke the next morning decidedly jaded, with a nasty taste in her mouth and a crashing headache. Ralph had warned her she would feel vile, and it served her right for drinking so much champagne.

With the windows so high, little light filtered in, and it was impossible to know what the time was. There was no noise from the dressing room, so she assumed Sally was not yet on duty, which must mean the hour was still early. However, she was wide awake, and wished to find herself a soothing tisane to ease her headache.

She slipped out of bed and ignited a few candles from the glowing embers of the fire. She then tossed a scuttle full of coal into the grate and added a few logs. As she straightened, she noticed that the communicating door was slightly open, and thought she would see if Ralph was awake.

Just in case he wasn't, she pushed it open quietly, and stepped in without calling out or knocking. The bed was empty and the fire out. The room was unpleasantly cold. Where on earth was he? She rushed across and burst into his sitting room, skidding to a halt in shock when she saw her husband sprawled in a drunken stupor in an armchair in front of a dying fire.

Her immediate reaction was dismay, but then she recalled her appalling display the previous night and how he had looked after her without demure. She tiptoed across and carefully removed the empty decanter and glass from his hands. Then she quietly added kindling and coal to his fire and stood back, watching to see if it would catch.

After a few moments, the flames

spurted through the wood, and she was confident the room would soon be warm. Next, she returned to his bedroom and removed the comforter, and was about to drape it over his snoring figure: he looked so uncomfortable, but she was at a loss to know how to improve the situation without waking him.

From the flickering light of the one candle she'd brought with her, she stood and considered what she should do. There was a similar chair opposite, and she carefully half-dragged, half-carried it until it was placed in front of him. Then she picked up his legs and dropped them onto the seat of the second chair. Once the comforter was added and a cushion pushed behind his head, she was confident she'd done as much as she could.

She pulled the door closed behind her, but didn't push the bolts across. Her heart skipped a beat as she thought about what might happen next time he came through it.

9

It had taken all Ralph's self-control not to reach out and tumble Verity onto his lap. Feigning sleep when the most desirable woman he'd ever met was flitting about in her nightclothes within arm's reach, and sending heat pulsing towards all the right places, was all but impossible. Somehow he managed — but only just.

He unclenched his fists and almost groaned out loud. If he hadn't drunk so much brandy and passed out, he would be in her bed this minute, making love to her. He was tempted to go to bed, but didn't want her to come in to check on him and find he'd moved after she'd taken so much trouble to make him comfortable.

He settled himself and closed his eyes, hoping his discomfort would settle if he recited the names of the regiments he'd served alongside for many years. It did the trick, and soon he was drifting off to sleep. He was woken the following morning when Jenkins rudely kicked his feet from the chair.

'Wake up, Sir Ralph, there's trouble downstairs and you're needed,' Jenkins said urgently.

Ralph stumbled to his feet, his head still foggy from sleep and alcohol. His man held out a clean shirt and he pulled it over his head. 'What's wrong? Tell me as I wash — I can't go down half-asleep.'

'It's the reverend gentleman, sir; he's telling everybody to leave because the castle's home to the Devil, and you and Lady Elrick are in league with him.'

'Damn it to hell! I should have spoken to him last night. I'm not sure that telling the staff we're overrun with Viking warriors rather than Satan's spawn will improve the situation — but one can but try.'

There was no time to shave, but plunging his face into icy cold water had woken him up. He ran his fingers through his hair, hastily tied his neckcloth, added a waistcoat, and was then ready to ram his arms into his topcoat.

His pocket watch was still on the shelf, and he'd not looked at the clock, so had no idea of the hour. As he hurtled down the stairs the longcase clock struck seven. The hall was empty, but then there were not usually any footmen in attendance until much later.

'Where are they? Has the wretched man gone down to the servants' hall to harangue them?'

'He has, and his presence is causing chaos. Even Hodgson and Saxton are hanging on his every word — if you don't do something right smartish, I reckon they'll all leave, regardless of the weather and the fact that it's Christmas Eve.'

Ralph swore beneath his breath and headed to the wing of the castle that housed the servants' quarters. He could hear the curate ranting long before he could see him. The room was packed with staff, and apart from the men he'd brought with him, and the two that came with Verity, everyone else was here listening with rapt attention.

'How can you remain under this cursed roof on the eve of Christ's birthday? We must depart from this place immediately before you are forever damned by association with the Devil and his acolytes. Castle Elrick is a place of evil . . .'

He'd heard quite enough of this nonsense. Ralph threw open the staff room door and erupted into the chamber. His sudden appearance had the desired effect and Peters fell instantly silent.

'Jenkins, remove this person. Whatever the weather, he'll be leaving here directly.'

His valet shot forward and marched the curate from the room. Ralph surveyed the assembled crowd, who were now shifting uncomfortably from foot to foot and obviously wishing they were anywhere else but here.

'I don't pay you to listen to sermons when you should be working. You knew this place was haunted before you came to work here — why else do you think I pay you double the normal wages? The ghosts have made themselves known to me, and they wish us no harm.' He gave them a brief explanation of the Vikings' wishes, and the atmosphere had lightened somewhat by the time he'd finished.

He then glared around the room, and no one dared to meet his eyes. 'I shall be closing Castle Elrick and moving back to Gloucestershire as soon as the weather improves. If you wish to leave today, you will do so without references or wages. However, if you remain until Lady Elrick and I depart, then you will be paid what you're owed — and a handsome bonus besides.'

He spotted the butler lurking at the back and spoke directly to him. 'Hodgson, I expect everyone to be back at work and the house running smoothly within the hour. Those that choose to depart must do so immediately. I'll leave the matter in your hands.'

Not waiting for a response, Ralph marched out, managing not to swear until he reached the privacy of the passageway. He hoped his bracing talk had done the trick, but even if they all left, he was sure the castle would still be habitable with the help of the remaining men. Even grooms could turn their hands to cleaning and cooking if they had to.

Verity was waiting in the hall when he returned. 'Ralph, Jenkins told me what happened. Do you think they will leave?'

'I hope not, sweetheart; but we'll manage, whatever happens. Now, do you care to come with me whilst I eject the ridiculous curate from the castle?'

She smiled her heart-stopping smile and slipped her hand through his arm. 'At least the blizzard has passed and the sun's out. Are you intending for the poor man to walk the five miles to his home?'

'It would serve him right if he did, but we can return him in the sleigh.' He closed his hand over hers and pressed it gently. 'However, any members of staff who choose to abandon us the day before Christmas will have to make their own way.'

He expected her to protest at this callous statement, but instead she nodded. 'Absolutely right, my dear, they are leaving their positions and don't deserve special treatment. I'm sure if they follow in the path of the sleigh they will make a safe return.'

They reached the side door where Peters was standing, enveloped in his cloak, his overnight bag in one hand and his Bible in the other. Jenkins was firmly gripping his elbow. For such a small and insignificant fellow, he had far too much to say for himself and had caused a deal of trouble. The man would no doubt prosper and go far in his chosen profession.

Ralph considered trying to explain to the curate the difference between ghosts and the Devil, but decided to let the matter go. He nodded to Jenkins, who opened the door and propelled Peters through it.

'I'll travel with him, Sir Ralph; make sure he gets home without causing further trouble.'

'Good man. Let's hope not too many of the staff decide to follow him.'

The wind whistled into the passageway and he slammed the door shut. 'There, he's gone. I'm not sure if we're going to get any breakfast, but we could light the candles in the garlands whilst we wait and see.'

* * *

Verity was very hungry indeed, and sincerely hoped he was wrong about their breakfast. 'If nothing appears in the next hour, I'll go down and make it myself. I'm a passable cook and an excellent housekeeper.'

'In which case I'd better brush up on my butlering skills and learn to serve at table. Then we have everything covered.'

It took half an hour to get all the candles burning in the great hall, but it was worth the effort. 'I've never seen anything so beautiful — it could be Prince Charming's Palace. I certainly feel like Cinderella.' The sound of hammering started up in the rooms that were being converted. 'Obviously the carpenters are still here — do you think we can move downstairs today?'

'I doubt it, sweetheart. It's likely we no longer have sufficient staff to get everything ready. I'm afraid you will have to remain where you are — for the moment, anyway.' Ralph had been helping her with her task, but now joined her in the centre under the mistletoe.

His wicked smile gave her fair warning of his intentions. 'You must not. We've not even had our breakfast!'

He ignored her feeble protest and

kissed her anyway. When he finally lifted his head, she was giddy with excitement, her lips tingled deliciously, and if she hadn't had his arms around her waist she would have sunk into a heap at his feet.

'Excuse me, Sir Ralph, my lady, but breakfast is served.' The butler was standing a few feet away with his surly expression.

She refused to be embarrassed by a servant. Instead of jumping out of Ralph's arms, she turned so her back was to him, but she remained within his embrace. 'Thank you, Hodgson, you may go about your duties now.'

He withdrew, his stance stiff, and she was glad he wouldn't be coming with them to Hertfordshire.

'Well done, sweetheart, about time he was put in his place. Shall we eat? Then you must summon the housekeeper, and we'll see how many have left.'

There was only one footman in attendance in the breakfast parlour, and only half the amount of dishes put out.

This didn't bode well.

She turned to the servant. 'I wish to speak to Saxton immediately. Has she remained on the premises?'

'No, my lady, she's left. There's Mr Hodgson, me, and one other footman left. I reckon all the women have gone.'

Verity's appetite deserted her. 'Ralph, however are we going to manage in this huge place for the next few weeks with nobody to cook and clean?'

He shrugged. 'Try living in the mountains in Spain in the middle of winter, my love; after that, everything is paradise. Come, let us eat before it gets unpalatable. We can worry about everything else after we're replete.'

Although there was little selection this morning, everything was perfectly cooked and quite delicious. Whoever had taken over in the kitchen was an excellent cook.

'I'll get everyone left together in the great hall — the outside men as well — then we can see how to divide out the work so we can all eat and live in relative comfort until we leave.' Ralph gestured to the footman, who vanished to convey his message.

Something occurred to her. 'I'm going upstairs to see if the two local girls who help Sally have stayed. They must also come down if they have.'

Jenkins was waiting to speak to Ralph, and her husband took her hand preventing her from leaving. 'Stay, sweetheart. I wish you to be involved in all the decisions regarding the running of Castle Elrick.'

'I reckon we'll manage right enough, sir, with those who remain. Morag, the scullery maid who got lost in the root cellars, has stayed, and her friend as well. It's they that cooked your breakfast. Hodgson wanted to leave, but ain't got nowhere else to go.'

Verity hurried off to fetch Sally, and hopefully the two chambermaids as well, leaving Jenkins and Ralph waiting in the hall for the remnants of the castle staff to arrive. She burst into her bedchamber and was delighted to find all three girls busy tidying.

'I'm so glad you're all here. You need to come downstairs immediately: there's going to be a staff meeting, and everyone must attend.'

Sally smiled, but the two girls looked nervous. 'We can manage up here and take care of your linen and such, so you'll not notice any difference. Should I continue with the packing for the move to your new rooms?'

Verity shook her head. 'Sir Ralph will now be moving in with me here — that will mean his man can get on with other duties. However, you three will have to take care of Sir Ralph's laundry as well as mine in future. Do you think you will be able to manage?'

'No trouble at all, my lady. We can give a hand in the kitchens as well when our duties here are done.'

'Thank you, your loyalty is much appreciated, and you will be amply remunerated.' She smiled at the other two. 'I don't know your names as yet, but if you intend to stay in my employ I would like to be able to address you correctly.'

Sally pointed to the slightly taller girl. 'That's Mary and the other is her sister, Ann.' The girls curtsied and looked slightly less unhappy.

'Welcome to my employ, Mary and Ann. I hope you will consider coming with us when we go to Gloucestershire.'

'Come with you? I reckon we would. Nothing here to keep us, that's for sure.' Mary beamed and her silent sister managed a weak smile.

'Excellent. Now, you must come downstairs immediately. Sir Ralph wishes to speak to everyone.'

She could hear the subdued murmur of voices before she was halfway down the staircase. She paused to view the great hall from above, delighted with the hundred flickering candles and the many garlands and wreaths that decorated the space.

There was already a satisfactory number of people milling about, exclaiming and pointing and enjoying the spectacle as much as she. From her vantage point, she quickly counted the number of females present, and was surprised to see that there were four, not just the two that Jenkins had mentioned.

Ralph beckoned her over and she ran to his side. 'We have ten outside men; six inside, if you include the two boot boys; and four maids. I gave Hodgson ten guineas and he was delighted to follow the others. I sent him in the sleigh with the curate and the luggage that couldn't be carried by hand.'

'That was kind of you. I'm glad he's gone; now we know that all who have remained wish to be here. We also have my abigail and two chambermaids to add to that number. If we close all the reception rooms apart from the breakfast parlour and the study, I can see no difficulty.'

The motley group continued to chatter amongst themselves, evidently not overawed to be in the great hall with their master and mistress so close by. The folk in the north of the country were obviously quite different from those in the south, who would have removed their outside footwear and be standing in nervous silence.

Ralph raised his hand, and to her astonishment everybody stopped talking and turned to face him. How had he done that when she was sure many of them had had their backs to him?

'Lady Elrick and I would like to thank you for your loyalty, and can assure you it will not go unrewarded. All of you that are here will have positions in Gloucestershire if you wish to come with us when we leave. If you don't, then you will have an excellent reference and sufficient funds to tide you over until you find another post.'

This announcement was greeted with a chorus of approval and a spontaneous round of applause. When this died away, Ralph stepped back and indicated that she should go with him, leaving Jenkins to complete the meeting.

Once they were snug in the study, he swept her into his arms again and spun her round as if she were a child. When he put her down, he kept hold of her hand and led her to the deep-seated chesterfield. 'This is going to be the best Christmas I've ever had. Jenkins is taking on the role of butler-cum-housekeeper — he'll soon have everything organised satisfactorily. Although he works as my valet he's always been in my confidence, and I trust him absolutely.'

She snuggled into his arms, enjoying the feeling of being loved and protected for the first time in her life. Her father had never been at home long enough to demonstrate his affection; she'd had to make do with his infrequent letters. These had always been loving and full of encouragement, but that was no substitute for physical affection.

'I'm not happy with little Morag and her friend being left with all the cooking — I do hope Jenkins finds someone willing to help them.'

He chuckled and dropped a kiss on top of her head. 'There will be more than one of the outside men only too happy to become kitchen assistants, and don't forget we still have the two boot boys. I've suggested everyone moves into the house, even the grooms: it will be easier to feed them all that way.'

'I just hope the ghosts remain invisible, for I doubt even the most loyal of your retainers would wish to remain if they actually came face-to-face with a Viking.'

She'd expected a laughing reply; when he didn't respond immediately, she twisted round to stare at him. Her stomach turned unpleasantly and she wished she'd not eaten so much breakfast.

'I wasn't going to tell you what happened last night, but I think I must. The ghosts are not as benevolent as we thought. They are able to move objects — if we don't do as they want, then I fear they might attack us.'

Her head spun at the awful possibility of axes and swords flying through the air with a life of their own. 'We should have realised this before. You were moved from the stairwell by them, were you not?' She shuddered and his arms tightened. 'How can we find their remains whilst the snow's still so deep?'

'There's the rub — I've no idea — and there's unlikely to be a thaw before March at the earliest. Once winter gets a hold it doesn't let go easily. Normally we would have been snowed in by November; I believe it might have been God's will that it remained clement until you were able to join me.'

'In which case, my love, we must put our faith in him again. If indeed he did bring me here, then he must have a solution to this problem and will present it to us when the time is right.'

He was staring at her in a most peculiar way. Surely those weren't tears glistening in his eyes? She was about to ask him what was bothering him when his expression changed. She'd never seen anyone look so happy.

10

'I can't believe you've just called me 'my love'. I've been liberally sprinkling my conversation with endearments, but this is the first time you've reciprocated. Does this mean you're beginning to feel the same way about me?'

'The same way? Are you telling me that it's not merely desire that's behind your shows of affection?'

'Initially, I was driven purely by lust. I still can't believe that such a beautiful woman wishes to share my bed.' He shook his head and brushed his hand across his eyes. 'It's ridiculous, incredible even, to be talking about feelings when we've only known each other for two days, but it's true. You are heaven-sent and I've fallen irrevocably in love with you.'

'And I with you — I wish this to be a true marriage. Papa has guided us together and must have known we would be an ideal match.' She could scarcely put one word after another, she was so bemused by what he'd said. A little over a week ago she had been living miserably with her stepmother and unpleasant half-sisters and now she was married to the most wonderful man in the world. 'I took the liberty of telling my maid that you would be sleeping in my bedchamber in future. I take it that's acceptable?'

His eyes darkened and the hectic flush she'd come to recognise coloured his cheekbones. 'Wild horses wouldn't keep me away, my darling, and I suggest we retire immediately after dinner.'

She couldn't stop her glance straying to the overmantel clock and was disappointed to see the time was only ten o'clock — at least eight hours before they could respectably retire. Unless she found something to occupy her time, she would go mad with longing.

'We must discover a way of satisfying the ghosts before they become violent.

Do you think there might be a ledger or diary written by one of your ancestors that could tell us where they were buried?'

He tipped her rudely from his lap and was on his feet before she'd finished her sentence. 'That's a brilliant notion, sweetheart, why didn't I think of it? We'll start searching the shelves in here first, and if we have no luck we can move to the library. Hopefully we'll find what we want before the time is up and trouble starts.'

'I'll start at this end of the bookcase and you start at the other. You'll have to investigate the top shelves as I cannot reach them without a set of steps.'

He stood back and surveyed the shelves. 'We can ignore the more recent books, the ones properly bound — what we want will be far more primitive . . . ' He stopped and smashed his fist into the wall, sending a cloud of plaster flying out. 'God's teeth! We're both fools. The Vikings were here more than one thousand years ago — I doubt that anyone could read and write in those days, and even if they could, nothing would have survived for so long.'

'How silly of me to think we could find any evidence after so many years.' She sat dejectedly on the nearest chair, at a loss to know what to suggest they do next. 'Do you think it possible these ghosts have appeared to your ancestors over the centuries?'

'They certainly have, that's why the place was abandoned over a hundred years ago. Why do you ask?'

'I was wondering if the occupants of Castle Elrick at that time might have recorded something that would help us.'

'Of course; they left in an almighty hurry, that's for sure. When I reoccupied the place three years ago, everything was left as if the occupants had just gone away for a week or so and intended to return. The furniture, fittings and so on were not taken.'

He gestured at the antique bookshelves filled with hundreds of old books. 'All these were here and I've not bothered to investigate any of them. It's possible there might be a diary or something similar, but I doubt we'll find it in here.' He frowned and then smiled. 'When I had the housekeeper prepare your apartment, there were several trunks of old books removed; but I've no idea where they went, and now Saxton has gone and we cannot ask her.'

'But we can go and search for ourselves. It's unlikely they were transported very far. There must be a dozen empty chambers upstairs they could have been moved to.'

Eventually they discovered the trunks of books in the fourth chamber they went into. 'It's too cold to remain in here and search, Verity, I'll get a couple of men to drag the trunks into your sitting room. Why don't you wait there for me?'

'I'll investigate each one. Maybe it will be possible to narrow down our search so all these don't have to be moved.'

None of the rooms had bell-straps, as they'd been built long before the days when ringing for your servant had become commonplace. Fortunately, the trunks were not stacked one on top of the other but put side by side, so she could look inside each one.

The first one she opened was full of dusty cushions and other fabric items. She slammed the lid back down. This left four still to look into. She was dusty and cold by the time she reached the fourth trunk, but at least she'd managed to eliminate the other three as holding nothing of interest to them.

Ralph appeared at the door and grinned down at her. 'Good grief, you're filthy.' He reached out and pulled her to her feet. 'Has your search been successful?'

'It has indeed. These two trunks are full of books, ledgers and other papers; the others have nothing of interest.' She shook off the worst of the dust from her skirts and smiled ruefully. 'There's little point in repairing the damage to my appearance until we've completed our search.'

'Your hands are icy, you mustn't remain here a moment longer. Jenkins is organising someone to fetch the trunks to us.' His smile was wolfish. 'I can think of a delightful way to warm you up.'

She couldn't prevent her cheeks from turning scarlet. 'We will both behave with decorum until the appropriate time. Remember, today is the eve of our Lord's birthday, and we should be thinking pure thoughts.'

He laughed and grabbed her hand, obviously not bothered by the grubby state of it. 'I've been thinking, sweetheart, we could attend midnight Mass in the village if you would care to. The weather's perfect for the sleigh.'

'I can think of nothing I'd like better. I've never travelled in a sleigh, and it would be a wonderful way to celebrate Christmas.'

★   ★   ★

The first trunk proved to have nothing relevant to their search within its confines. A tray appeared at midday with sandwiches and coffee, and they paused in their task in order to enjoy the refreshments. Ralph was regretting his impulsive offer to escort Verity to church, for this now meant they couldn't retire to bed immediately after dinner. The thought of waiting even a few hours longer to make love to his wife was driving him insane.

Crouching beside her whilst they examined each item in the first trunk had been torture. He was desperate to consummate the union — until he'd done so, he was still afraid she might change her mind and demand to be released from the arrangement.

Why should such a lovely girl wish to remain with a ruined wreck of a man like himself? She wasn't interested in his wealth or title — so what on earth had prompted her to fall in love with him? Unable to remain in the same room as her without picking her up and carrying her to his bed, he stood up and brushed his hands down his breeches.

'I'm going to check everything's running smoothly downstairs. I also want to make sure the sleigh took no damage yesterday when it returned the curate to his home.'

She looked up with a smile and brushed aside a strand of hair that had fallen from the neat arrangement at the back of her neck. Doing so left a trail of dirt across her cheek. 'There are only a dozen or so items left in this last trunk, I can examine them myself. I fear we're not going to find anything that will be of help. I do hope that these ghosts of yours will remain harmless until after Twelfth Night — that should give us ample time to come up with a way to find the burial site.'

Somehow he kept his smile in place. 'I'm sure they will, my love. Now, pray excuse me. I'll be in the study later if you want me, or if you find anything of interest.'

He couldn't ruin her happiness by revealing they only had until the end of

Christmas Day to find the bones, that all of them could be in mortal danger from that point forward. He was no more than a few strides from the door when he heard her shriek.

He was at her side in seconds, his heart hammering. 'What is it? Have you found something?'

She held up a slim, leather-bound book. 'It's in here.' She held it up in order to show him the front cover. 'See, Ralph, the title tells us this is what we're looking for.'

He read the faded gold lettering: *A Detailed History of the Viking Attack on Castle Elrick.*

'Have you had time to read it?'

'No, I've only just found it.' She scrambled to her feet and rushed across to the side table where there was more light filtering in from the windows. Her hands were trembling and she was having difficulty turning the pages.

'Let me, you're overwrought, my love.' Obediently she handed him the book. He pulled up a straight-backed chair so he could sit close to her, then placed the volume between them whilst he read the introduction. The language was old-fashioned, the black print sadly faded, but he could decipher sufficient to know this was the answer to their prayers.

She had been reading as well, and looked up at him, her eyes shining with joy. 'See, Chapter Eight is entitled: *The Rude Burial of the Invaders*. I can hardly bear to look! Turn to the page so we can read it together.'

'God's teeth! How could I not have realised this is where they lie? I've walked past that place a dozen times, and wondered why there are strange markings on the castle wall.'

Now he could tell her the ultimatum the Viking had given him. She was remarkably calm about his announcement. No wringing of hands, sighs or sobbing — there couldn't be another girl in the land who was so sensible and brave, and so absolutely adorable.

To his astonishment she made an

extraordinary suggestion. 'We must go at once and tell them the good news. Then they can prepare themselves for the journey to their own spiritual home whilst we celebrate Christ's birthday.'

He wasn't sure this was safe, but he could refuse her nothing. 'Very well, if you're quite sure you wish to encounter them again. There's something odd about all this, don't you think?'

'What do you mean?'

'Why have they not spoken to previous members of the family? They've been languishing here for centuries, have been seen about the place, and yet have waited until now to state their wishes?'

'That's another thing we must speak about when we meet them. What I find puzzling is that there appears to be more than one heaven — how can that be? Does this mean that our Christian teachings are untrue? Is there more than one god after all?'

'I've not given the matter much thought, sweetheart. I imagine that as these Viking fellows knew nothing about

Christianity, they worshipped in the best way they could — I don't see why there couldn't be a place for those that approached God in a different way to us. I seem to remember somewhere in the Bible a passage about there being many rooms in heaven.'

She nodded solemnly. 'That's exactly what I think. Now, shall we speak to your Vikings and give them the good news?'

* * *

Who could have imagined that one's life could have changed so dramatically in such a short space of time? Verity had never been so happy — she was the luckiest girl alive to have fallen in love so quickly with this wonderful man, and for him to reciprocate her feelings.

Everything else seemed insignificant in comparison to this. The ghosts would be pleased with their news, and they could celebrate Christmas without fear of being massacred in their beds. She shivered — not from fear of what these

Viking warriors might do, but in eager anticipation at what was going to take place in her bed that very night.

'Where do you think we'll have the best chance of finding them? Are we going to the strange door where we met them first?'

'They were in the study last time I saw them, so we shall go there.'

She stopped so suddenly her toes were squashed against the end of her slippers. 'You didn't say they came into our living space. I don't like the idea that they can move about at will and invade our privacy whenever they wish.'

He tightened his hold and swept her along willy-nilly. 'It's too late to become missish about this, my dear. The ghosts are quite capable of appearing anywhere in the castle: it's just that so far they've restricted themselves to the passageway, the backstairs and the study.'

'All I can say is that I'm glad we're moving away as soon as the weather allows us to, for I'll never be able to relax anywhere in this place after what you've told me.'

'Once the ghosts have gone, I can't see why we can't stay here. After all, it's my ancestral home.'

She drew breath to tell him in no uncertain terms what she thought of his suggestion when he chuckled. 'I don't take kindly to being made fun of, sir, especially about something as important as this.'

They had now reached the study and she hung back, hoping he'd changed his mind, but he propelled her forward and before she could say another word she was inside.

Both fires were burning and the room, with its garlands and candles, looked festive and cheerful. Perhaps she was being silly about this and should accept that the supernatural was beyond her comprehension and there was nothing she could do about any of it.

'They can read my thoughts, but I will speak aloud to them so that you know what's going on.' He stood in the middle of the room, shoulders back, his head slightly tilted and he'd never looked more brave or more handsome.

'We wish to speak to you. We have information pertinent to your request, and also a question we wish to be answered.'

For a minute or two, nothing happened, then the air seemed to shimmer and the flames flickered and almost went out. The room was much colder. She blinked. Was she seeing things, or was there a group of figures surrounding Ralph?

'Thank you for coming. I wish to tell you we now know where your mortal remains were buried and I've already got men clearing the snow. I have a suitable fishing boat we can put them in, and will use the swords from the wall of the great hall.'

The shapes flickered and he nodded. They must have replied but she couldn't hear them. He glanced towards her. 'They are pleased with the progress we've made and happy with the arrangements I've suggested. I'm going to ask them your question now.'

This time he didn't speak out loud, but she watched his expression closely, and saw the ghosts swirl around him for a moment and then vanish. Immediately the room was warm and the fire burned bright again.

'What did they say?'

'They said it wasn't until you arrived that the atmosphere was conducive to communication. For some reason you're a conduit to the afterworld. Hopefully we'll be able to send them on their way later today and can then enjoy a double celebration.' He saw her expression and hastily continued, 'I'm referring to the fact that we have just got married, nothing else.'

Reassured he'd meant no disrespect, she smiled. 'Is there anything I can do to help?'

He shook his head. 'Everything's in hand, sweetheart. However, I want you to be at my side when we ignite the boat and send it out to sea.'

'I wouldn't miss it for the world. This is something we can talk to our children and grandchildren about — I doubt they'll believe us, but it will certainly make a good tale.'

In two swift steps he was beside her and encircled her with his arms. 'I was wondering, my darling, if perhaps you might require an afternoon rest? The forthcoming excitement of sending our unwanted visitors on their fiery way and our sleigh ride to the village in the middle of the night will be rather tiring.'

11

Verity almost agreed with his outrageous suggestion, but this would mean Sally and the girls would be well aware why they had been sent away. 'Absolutely not! I shall retire at the proper time and not a moment sooner.'

He nibbled her ear, sending ripples of pleasure all the way to her toes. 'I didn't expect you to agree, sweetheart, but I thought it was worth asking.' He released her, but not before stealing a kiss. 'I'm going to see how the search is progressing. There's no need for you to come out until everything's in place.'

'Do you trust these beings to leave without causing harm to any of us?' For some reason, despite the evidence to the contrary, she was worried something catastrophic would happen.

'I don't think it's possible to trust a ghost, my love; but they've been here so long and never actually harmed anyone, so why should they do so now?'

'I don't know, but they might want revenge for all the years they've been trapped here.'

'I'd hope they would be thankful, not angry. Anyway, whatever happens, Castle Elrick will be free of unwanted guests by this evening.'

The hammering in the downstairs apartment had ceased and Verity went to investigate the reason for this. She pushed open the door and was delighted to find the partition wall had already been constructed, the door was in place, and several items of furniture had been fetched. These downstairs windows had inside shutters as well as curtains, so once the bedchamber was completed they could move in.

The new door opened smoothly and she walked through. This too was empty of labourers, but sadly their tools and debris were everywhere. Ralph was right — they wouldn't be moving in for a few days. Presumably the carpenters had been summoned to help dig up the bones, or make sure the boat was seaworthy.

Although disappointed she would spend her first night as a wife in the depressing room upstairs, Verity was certain what would take place between her and Ralph would be just as exciting wherever it happened. The castle seemed strangely quiet with so few members of staff remaining, but perhaps this was a good thing in view of the unusual circumstances.

Sally greeted her with enthusiasm and a strange request. 'Everyone's talking about sending the bones out to sea in a burning ship just like they did all those years ago. We'd like to watch, if Sir Ralph would allow us to.'

'I think that would be a splendid notion. Everybody must come out and form a burial party. This will demonstrate that we respect their traditions even if we don't believe in them ourselves. I'll go down and speak to Sir Ralph now and make sure he's agreeable. I shall need my warmest cloak, gloves and muffler when I return. You will need to dress warmly as well if you're allowed to come out.'

Ralph was nowhere to be found, but Verity discovered Jenkins returning from the stables. She explained why she was searching for her husband.

'The matter's in hand, my lady. I was just coming in to bring you the message. It'll be almost dark by then, and mighty slippery on the rocks. Sir Ralph wants everyone to meet in the courtyard in a quarter of an hour. There'll be sufficient torches to be able to see.'

'No wonder inside is deserted: the staff are getting ready, and so must I.'

In less than the allotted time, Verity led her three maids out into the courtyard. The space was alight with flambeaux and the golden glow reflected on the snow, giving the area a party atmosphere. No doubt the servants would be as pleased as she and Ralph would be when the Vikings finally left Castle Elrick.

She picked him out immediately, even in the semi-darkness, as he was a head taller than anyone else. He was deep in conversation with Jenkins, but he seemed to sense she was there as he glanced across. The flash of white teeth was all she could discern, but then he strode across to her.

'It's going to be difficult and somewhat dangerous getting to the beach, sweetheart, but we've rigged up some ropes for everyone to hang onto as they go down. Are you ready? The bones are in the boat, and we've piled the swords and bundles of firewood in on top of them. The funeral boat should really be lit by a blazing arrow, but we'll have to make do with a slow fuse.'

'I'm glad this is being done before Christmas Day — best to get the pagan celebrations out of the way first.' He took her arm and pulled it through his, and together they led the way round the castle to the seaward side — somewhere she'd not yet visited.

The hood of her cloak was blown back by an icy gust of salt-laden wind, and the torch she was holding flickered and almost went out. He pulled her closer to his side. 'I should have warned you it would be much colder here. It's a ten-minute walk along the shingle, and then we climb down to the sea.'

She barely heard his words, as they were blown away by the wind and drowned by the noise of the waves crashing on the rocks a short distance from them. When she reached the ropes that would guide her down to the beach, she was regretting her impulsive decision. Her fingers were numb, her toes also, and she couldn't keep her cloak closed around her.

'I'll go ahead of you, Verity; you keep one hand on my shoulder, and with the other hold tight onto the rope.'

Somehow she managed to negotiate the difficult descent without mishap, and quickly moved away to allow the others to follow. The small fishing boat had been rigged with a sail which was flapping madly in the wind in an effort to tear itself away from the mast. The interior of the boat was invisible: all she could see were the bundles of logs.

'Come along, we've moved some rocks so everyone can stand safely where the waves won't reach. The tide is on the ebb, perfect for our task as it will carry the boat out to sea.'

'Do you think the ghosts are already on the boat, or still inside watching us from the window?'

'How should I know? I'm not an expert on the subject, sweetheart, but hopefully they'll join their mortal remains as soon as the boat's aflame.'

In less than a quarter of an hour, every living soul had left Castle Elrick to gather on the rocky shore. Ralph stood beside her, his arm firmly around her waist, and she was glad of his strength and warmth. Despite his reassurances she kept looking nervously over her shoulder at the castle, and was almost certain she'd seen a strange flickering at several of the windows.

No apparent signal was given, but Jenkins and two others pushed the boat away from shore. Immediately the sail billowed and filled with air, and the boat sped away from the shore as if pushed by invisible hands. There was a faint glow in the stern, and suddenly the vessel was engulfed in flames.

A collective sigh of appreciation rippled around the gathered crowd, and for a moment six Viking warriors were clearly visible holding their weapons above their heads amidst the flames.

'Did you see that? They've gone — we've given them what they want.' Verity sagged against him in relief and he hugged her.

Then someone at the back screamed. She was spun round, and her knees almost gave way beneath her. The castle was in flames. There was a general surge forward as the men began to scramble up the rocks. Ralph abandoned her and raced forward.

* * *

Verity had been right to worry about revenge. Somehow the Vikings had managed to start a fire inside and from the look of it the flames had taken hold throughout the lower floor. Thank God they'd all come out to watch.

'Stay where you are! Nobody goes near the fire. It's too late to save your possessions, and I don't give a damn about the building.' His voice, at parade-ground volume, carried above the waves and the wind.

The three men about to scramble up the rocks remained where they were. Jenkins panted up beside him.

'Buggeration! We'll not put that out in a hurry, sir. We'd better get to the stables to make sure the nags are not panicking.'

'You four go ahead and see to the horses — I'll oversee the ascent and make sure nobody is harmed.' He turned to the dozen or so people remaining on the beach. Verity was walking among them offering comfort and reassurance. He beckoned her over.

'I hope you have nothing of sentimental value in your apartment, sweetheart. I'll replace everything else, but personal

items will be incinerated in the confla-
gration.'

'I have everything I want right here,
Ralph, and as long as you're safe I shall
be content.'

Despite the catastrophe, he wanted to
punch his fist in the air and roar his
triumph into the night sky. Fortunately,
he managed to restrain this impulse, as
there'd been more than enough excitement already. He gathered her close
and, ignoring the interested spectators,
kissed her thoroughly. When he raised
his head, he could see from the light of
the fire she was as happy as he.

'I love you, and promise I'll make you
happy and that you'll never regret your
decision to marry me.'

She smiled and nodded towards their
servants. 'We must get everybody safely
to the stables. We can sleep there tonight.
Not only will it be warm, but appropriate when you consider the date, don't
you think?'

By the time they reached the courtyard, the castle was well ablaze and it

was difficult to breathe comfortably in the swirling smoke. Jenkins appeared, his muffler around his mouth.

'It's only a matter of time before the fire gets into the stables, sir. We'd best evacuate to the village. The horses are tacked and the sleigh and carriage ready. I reckon the ladies can travel in comfort, but everyone else will have to ride.'

Ralph turned to speak to his wife, but she'd vanished, and for a dreadful moment he couldn't see her. Then she appeared leading her magnificent stallion, which was already saddled. 'I'll ride Star — he has his rug on and will be fine in the snow. I hope the village hostelry can accommodate all of us.'

The horse reared, lifting her off her feet, and Ralph was about to leap forward when she calmed the beast. They had to get out of here before they were overcome by the smoke and the horses too terrified to be ridden or driven safely.

He grabbed Verity and tossed her

into the saddle of her massive mount. 'Ride across the moat and wait in the shelter of the walls. You'll be safe enough there until we can join you. We won't go to the village, but ride to our nearest neighbours, who will be in a better position to take us in than the Goat & Boot in the village.'

He watched her expertly guide her horse through the archway to safety, and then turned his attention to getting everyone else away from danger. All the horses were rugged and the spare blankets had been shared amongst those in the sleigh who would be coldest.

His own mount was skittering nervously on the cobbles, despite his firm hold on the bit. Jenkins appeared beside him. 'That's everyone out — including three cats and a terrier. We can go now, sir.'

Ralph vaulted into the saddle and guided his horse out to join the others. There were lamps bobbing about on the carriage and sleigh, and several of the men still had their torches. More than enough light to guide them to their destination. He made his way to the front where Verity waited, magnificent on her horse.

'We're going to Dunwoody Manor. The Rutherford family live there and I'm sure they'll be able to take us all in. The house is massive — he's a wealthy industrialist — so it will be far better than going to the village.'

'Is it a difficult route? Isn't there a danger we will become stuck in the snow?'

'We have to go back the way you came a few days ago, but instead of going towards the village we turn right and head inland. It's a well-used road and there should be no difficulty as others will have found the safest path already.'

They had been travelling for no more than three quarters of an hour, making reasonable headway considering the conditions, when Jenkins cantered back to join them. He'd been scouting ahead, making sure the route was possible for the little cavalcade.

'I've sent a man to warn Mr Rutherford that we're coming. You can see the lights of the Manor when we reach the brow of this hill. I don't reckon it's more than a mile or two.'

* * *

Verity had been impressed by the speed and efficiency with which her husband and his man had organised everything. It must come from being soldiers, for she was certain no ordinary gentleman could have done so.

From Star's back, she could see further than most, and was becoming increasingly concerned about the way the snow was blowing in their direction. Although it wasn't actually a fresh fall, there was so much lying in the fields either side of the lane that it would soon make the route impassable.

She was about to mention her worries to Ralph when Jenkins arrived, bringing the excellent news that they had almost reached their destination. She turned her horse and rode him back to the sleigh where she told the girls they would soon be safe and warm inside.

'Don't worry about us, my lady; we've not been in a sleigh before, and we feel ever so grand. With all these blankets over our knees, we're hardly cold at all,' Sally called out cheerfully.

In fact, everybody was remarkably sanguine about being homeless and with not a change of clothes amongst them. Certainly Ralph had accepted the destruction of his ancestral home as if it was of no more consequence than a garden bonfire.

Confident the message would travel to all members of the party, Verity returned to her position next to her husband. 'See, darling, the house is ablaze with lights, and if I'm not mistaken there are a couple of horsemen galloping this way. This isn't how I intended us to spend our wedding night, but we must make the best of it.'

The remainder of the journey seemed endless, and when eventually she trotted Star into the turning circle she was eager to dismount and get into the house. Ralph dismounted first and turned to lift her from the saddle.

'Mrs Rutherford is waiting to greet you, my love; rooms are being prepared for us and accommodation made ready for our staff. I shall join you as soon as I'm sure my people and the horses are comfortable.'

A stout lady of middle years, wearing an extraordinary turban, bustled down the marble steps and held out her hands in greeting. 'Lady Elrick, what a thing to happen! And on Christmas Eve, too. Come in, come in, my dear, and let us get you warm and dry.'

Verity was too exhausted to do more than nod and smile in the appropriate places. She was guided through a vast entrance hall and up the equally huge marble staircase. Everywhere she looked there were gilded cherubs and pink marble pillars. This was a modern house, and more luxurious than anywhere she'd ever set foot in before.

'Here you are, my dear Lady Elrick, my daughters have donated sufficient garments to keep you going until you can replenish your wardrobe. Unfortunately, your husband is a head taller than Mr Rutherford, so I've no idea how we shall be able to clothe him . . . '

'I'm sure we will manage, thank you, Mrs Rutherford. It's so kind of you to take us all in like this . . . '

'Think nothing of it, my lady, there's nothing I like better than entertaining, and my son and his family were due to spend the festive season with us but could not come because of the snow. You are very welcome. Will you dine with us or do you wish to have trays sent up?'

For a moment Verity was unable to think of an answer. With so much happening, she had thought the hour much later, and that dinner would have been eaten long ago. 'I should love to dine with you; I'll be down as soon as I can. Thank you so much.'

The two girls allocated to her stripped off her cold, wet garments in minutes, and had her back into a clean gown before she'd had time to see what they were putting on her. Her hair was dressed and a soft cashmere shawl placed around her shoulders.

'There, my lady, you look as pretty as a picture, if you don't mind me saying so. That gown never looked so fine on Miss Rutherford, and it's her favourite.'

This was hardly an appropriate thing to say, but she let it go with a smile. The girl stepped aside, allowing Verity to see herself for the first time in the full-length mirror. Good grief! She'd never seen so many ribbons and rouleau in her life — and the fabric was a hideous shade of puce, which did nothing to improve it.

She wasn't sure whether to laugh or cry, but then she saw the expectant faces of the girls who obviously thought this was a magnificent ensemble. 'Thank you so much, this fits perfectly. Is there a footman outside who can show me the way? For I'm sure I shall get lost in this huge house!'

The girl who'd spoken dipped in a small curtsy. 'I'll take you myself, my lady; we don't stand on ceremony here. The missis is ever so pleased to be having such grand folk as you staying here, I can tell you.'

By some miracle Ralph had managed to repair his appearance, and although not in evening dress, he still looked smart. His eyebrows shot under his hair when he saw her approaching, but he managed to hide his astonishment at her outfit by coughing into his hand.

'I know, it's hideous, but it fits; and it's very kind of Miss Rutherford to lend me her best gown,' she murmured to him when she was close enough not to be overheard.

After the introductions to the remainder of the family had taken place, they were offered champagne and she didn't have the heart to refuse. She decided to be more careful this time, and not take a second glass.

Dinner was elaborate and rich, but delicious nonetheless. Mrs Rutherford rose at the end of the interminable meal, and Verity and the two daughters followed their hostess into the drawing room.

'That was quite the best meal I've ever eaten, Mrs Rutherford. Do you attend a midnight service tonight?'

'No, my lady, we have our own chapel — the vicar sends his curate on Christmas morning at nine o'clock, and we break our fast afterwards.'

'In which case, madam, I hope you will forgive me if I retire. It's been an exhausting and upsetting day, as you might imagine.'

'Of course, of course, I quite understand. I shall send a footman to guide you to your chamber.'

'Thank you, but I shall be able to find my way without assistance. I took note of the paintings and statues I passed, and it should be sufficient.'

All three ladies curtsied to her, which she found rather unsettling; she smiled and nodded as was expected by someone of her elevated status. 'I bid you good night, Sir Ralph and I will be down promptly at nine o'clock to attend the service with you all.'

Finding her way back wasn't quite as simple as she'd anticipated, but eventually she was there, and delighted to find Sally and her assistants waiting to take care of her. She'd no idea where Ralph had been put, or if he knew where she was. However, he was a resourceful gentleman, and would no doubt find her soon when he came up.

She was in the lace-covered nightgown that had been provided for her, her hair had been brushed through, and she dismissed the girls. 'I shan't need you anymore tonight, Sally; go down and join in the festivities. Mrs Rutherford told me the servants have some sort of celebration tonight.'

'Thank you, my lady. We're sharing a room upstairs and it's ever so cosy and warm. We've fallen on our feet here, that's for sure.'

As Sally was whisking into the dressing room, she called back over her shoulder, 'Sir Ralph's next door, my lady, in case you were wondering.'

Verity heard the girls giggling as they left, and her cheeks burned. She saw the communicating door immediately, turned the pretty glass knob, and peeked in —

She was transfixed and forced to hold onto the door in order to remain upright.

Ralph was standing with his back to her, and he didn't have a stitch of clothing on. He was unaware of her arrival, which gave her time to stare. Her glance travelled from the thick dark hair that curled at the nape of his neck, across his broad, muscled shoulders, down to his narrow waist and . . . and . . . She couldn't continue her appraisal.

'Come in, darling, don't dither about in the doorway.' His voice was light, but the words made her catch her breath.

'I can't, I really can't, I'm going back but I'll leave the door open.'

She flung herself under the covers,

her heart beating so hard she thought it might jump from her chest. Until that moment she hadn't quite understood what would be involved. Somehow she'd thought they would both remain in their nightclothes — never in her wildest dreams had she considered they would be naked. Well, *he* might be naked, but *she* was certainly going to keep her nightdress on!

She kept her eyes closed as she had no wish to see any more of him than she had already. The bed dipped and she held her breath. Why didn't he speak to her? What was he doing? After an eternity, she turned her head and risked a quick glance.

He was lying next to her, his head propped on one hand and his eyes laughing. There was still no sign of a nightshirt. 'At last! For a dreadful moment, I thought you'd gone to sleep.'

'Of course I haven't, I was waiting for you, but . . . '

'Don't look so worried, my love; nothing is going to happen that you don't want. If you change your mind at any time, I'll understand and leave you on your own.'

She couldn't take her eyes away. Despite her fears, she wanted him to stay, wanted to feel his body close to hers and become his true wife. However, his lack of clothing bothered her.

'You have nothing on, Ralph, and I am wearing my nightdress.' She'd intended to tell him he must put his back on before they could proceed, but he interrupted.

He moved smoothly across so he was touching her. 'That situation is soon remedied, sweetheart, you must take yours off.'

She clutched the covers under her chin and shook her head vehemently. 'No, you must put yours back on.'

His expression changed. 'I should have realised — you don't want to see my disfigurement, and I don't blame you.' He rolled away from her and rose to his feet. 'Keep your eyes averted, my love; I'll come back decently clothed and we can begin again.'

That wasn't what she'd meant at all! She tumbled from the bed and ran after him. 'You're not disfigured, you are beautiful!' She flung her arms around his waist and kissed his shoulder. He tensed, and she thought she'd offended him again. She moved her fingers slowly along the wicked scars that ran from his left hip, across his belly and up under his ribs. They did not repulse her — they had the opposite effect.

'You don't mind? You don't think of me as a hideous beast? Have you seen my leg? Doesn't that repulse you?'

'Of course I don't. I've told you — I love you, and I want to be your wife.'

With what sounded like a groan he turned, his eyes blazed down into hers, and she forgot everything apart from wanting to be one with him.

He didn't ask her to raise her arms, but gripped the opening of her night-gown and ripped it from top to hem. The material fell to the floor, leaving her in the same condition as him. She wasn't embarrassed any more, but revelled in their closeness. He scooped her up, and in two strides reached his bed and tossed her unceremoniously into the centre.

He joined her, and when his bare thigh touched hers she forgot everything and lost herself in a world of sensation and exquisite pleasure.

Later on, as she lay contented in his arms, she heard a distant church bell ring out for Christmas Day. 'Merry Christmas, my darling Ralph. I never believed I could be as happy as I am at this moment.'

He pushed away a strand of her hair from her cheek and kissed her tenderly. 'I love you, Verity, and in the morning we shall celebrate Christ's birthday and give thanks that we have found each other.'

We do hope that you have enjoyed reading this large print book.

Did you know that all of our titles are available for purchase?

We publish a wide range of high quality large print books including:
Romances, Mysteries, Classics
General Fiction
Non Fiction and Westerns

Special interest titles available in large print are:
The Little Oxford Dictionary
Music Book, Song Book
Hymn Book, Service Book

Also available from us courtesy of Oxford University Press:
Young Readers' Dictionary
(large print edition)
Young Readers' Thesaurus
(large print edition)

For further information or a free brochure, please contact us at:
Ulverscroft Large Print Books Ltd.,
The Green, Bradgate Road, Anstey,
Leicester, LE7 7FU, England.
Tel: (00 44) **0116 236 4325**
Fax: (00 44) **0116 234 0205**

SECRETS OF MELLIN COVE

Rena George

After Wenna discovers a shocking family secret, she flies to the comfort of her beloved Cornish moors. What can she do? If she reveals the terrible truth, her family will be ruined. If she does nothing, she could be condemning the crew of a sailing ship to death. Perhaps she should confide in the tall stranger who rides past her every day, always casting an interested glance in her direction. But would he understand, or would he go straight to the authorities? No, she couldn't trust a stranger . . . or could she?

RUNAWAY LOVE

Fay Wentworth

When Emma flees to Leigh Manor to escape the pain of a broken romance, she finds that life there as a secretary to Alex Baron is not as simple as she anticipated. An unfortunate encounter between herself, Alex and a bull heralds the start of a fiery relationship. And what is the mystery behind the charming façade of Blake, Alex's assistant? As Emma's new job gets off to a rocky start, she soon finds herself wondering who she can trust — and whether coming to Leigh Manor was a good idea . . .

GIFT OF THE NILE

Heidi Sullivan

Amber Davis has always loved hearing about her father's archaeological excavations, and is thrilled when she is finally allowed to accompany the professor on an expedition. As she begins her Egyptian adventure, she meets expatriates Lachlan and his son James. Amber is drawn to the artistic and bohemian James, but is concerned about the lecherous eye of his father. When things begin to go very wrong during the trip, can Amber keep her head . . . and her heart?

TRUSTING A STRANGER

Sarah Purdue

Clara Radley's life is all about her studies until she is woken in the night by hammering on her front door. Into her world steps handsome US Special Agent Jack Henry, who tells her that her life is in danger and his job is to protect her. Henry has been sent by her biological father — a US Army General who Clara has never even met. How can she trust this stranger? But what choice does she have?

THE TREGELIAN HOARD

Ellie Holmes

With her engagement in tatters, Jonquil Jones, a Portable Antiquities specialist, moves to Cornwall for a fresh start. When a golden torc that has lain hidden underground for centuries is unearthed, she can feel her soul stirring with excitement. Is it a single find, or part of an extraordinary treasure trove? It's Jonquil's job to find out. But there is one problem: Sebastian Ableyard, who reported the find, is the man Jonquil holds responsible for the break-up of her engagement . . .